THEY COULD NOT CONTAIN THEMSELVES

Advance Praise for

THEY COULD NO LONGER CONTAIN THEMSELVES

"It's often said if you want to get a true feel for a story writer's work you need to read at least one entire collection by that writer. The Rose Metal Press chapbooks speed this up. With a collection of *collections* like *They Could No Longer Contain Themselves*, you begin to get a feel for an entire generation of writers."

—Robert Shapard, coeditor of *Sudden Fiction Latino*

"What a fantastic collection. Wow! What emerges is the sense of the possibilities of compression and conviction, each piece complete in itself, connected to the whole. Throughout is Jodzio's 'tiny spark, that small bit of combustion deep inside,' a desire that demands our intense attention, that, to rephrase Colen, might steal breath back if we look away. It's all so full of wonder and surprise, where purple thermoses meet the edge of sky, couples spread arms and fingers to quantify love, and Charlie Brown, in 'this same musty shirt, 34 years,' writes it all down."

—Randall Brown, author of *Mad to Live*

"Rose Metal Press has done it again. A wonderful range of voices comes at you from this collection of flash fictions with stories that haunt, that tell of grit and love and loss and longing with the kind of detail and patience that makes your teeth ache."

—Sherrie Flick, author of *I Call This Flirting*

THEY COULD NO LONGER CONTAIN THEMSELVES

A Collection of Five Flash Chapbooks

: ELIZABETH J. COLEN :

: JOHN JODZIO :

: TIM JONES-YELVINGTON :

: SEAN LOVELACE :

: MARY MILLER :

Rose Metal Press

2011

Rose Metal Press, Inc.
P.O. Box 1956
Brookline, MA 02446
rosemetalpress@gmail.com
www.rosemetalpress.com

Library of Congress Cataloging Information: 2011926890

ISBN: 978-0-9846166-1-9

Cover and interior design by Heather Butterfield
See "A Note About the Type" for more information about the typefaces used.

Cover art: *Sucking or Blowing*, by Ethan Hayes-Chute
More information and images can be viewed at his website: www.ethanhc.com.

This book is manufactured in the United States of America and printed on acid-free paper.

Table of Contents

Preface

In 2009, celebrity judge Sherrie Flick chose Sean Lovelace's *How Some People Like Their Eggs* as the winner of our Third Annual Short Short Chapbook Contest. Flick said of the book, "Lovelace's little stories seek out these big-guy concepts and bring them down like in an old movie filled with gangsters, trench coats, cigarettes, and tough-talking women with nice legs—using smart dialogue and wit." Lovelace's chapbook spoke to more than just Flick: By spring 2010, the run of 300 specialty letterpressed copies of *Eggs* was on the verge of selling out.

Around this same time we heard from our Fourth Annual Contest judge Dinty W. Moore that he'd chosen Mary Hamilton's *We Know What We Are* as the 2010 winner. We were thrilled, but found ourselves loath to give up the other four finalists—Elizabeth J. Colen's *Dear Mother Monster, Dear Daughter Mistake,* John Jodzio's *Do Not Touch Me Not Now Not Ever,* Tim Jones-Yelvington's *Evan's House and the Other Boys Who Live There,* and Mary Miller's *Paper and Tassels*—to other publishers. All five of the finalists that year stunned us with their precision and heart, their longing and skill. It was the most stylistically diverse group of finalists we'd ever had, and yet all the manuscripts hummed with the same kind of energy and deep humanness. We had to publish them.

And so we decided to bring the four finalists from our Fourth Annual Short Short Contest and the celebrated and sold-out winner of our third together under one cover.

"The ceiling began to leak, the water accumulating on the table. I lit a cigarette and smoked it while watching the drops swell and swell until they could no longer contain themselves." These are the last two lines of Mary Miller's story "Aesthete," narrated by a teenage girl who wants to push boundaries and connect, but ultimately remains closed off from her companions. We chose to title this collection *They Could No Longer Contain Themselves* because, for all the differences in writing style, technique, and theme, the characters throughout these five chapbooks are barely contained and bursting out. They form a chorus of voices that vibrate with both the desire to break free of the relationships that hold them, hurt them, and define them, and the desire to more deeply entwine themselves into the lives of others to fend off ever-threatening loneliness, isolation, and self-loathing.

But Colen, Jodzio, Jones-Yelvington, Lovelace, and Miller don't let their stories get bogged down in all that pulsing intensity. They harness the absurd, they write great dialogue, they make you wince and laugh—they are all masters of our favorite kind of story, one that is funny and sad at the same time.

—Abigail Beckel & Kathleen Rooney
Rose Metal Press
March 2011

Do Not Touch Me Not Now Not Ever

: *by John Jodzio* :

Acknowledgments

"Mail Game" *In Posse Review*
"Inventory" *Bullfight Review*
"The Dojo" *Pindeldyboz*
"My First Wife" *MNArtists.org*
"Octane" *Pindeldyboz*
"The Two Malls" *Twelve Stories*
"Do Not Touch Me Not Now Not Ever" *Monkeybicycle*
"Guns and Gold" *deComp*
"Shoo, Shoo" *MNArtists.org*
"Vessels" *Pindeldyboz*

Table of Contents

Mail Game

.....

I was playing this mail game with a girl at work.

Hot potato, basically.

Except it was with this two-dollar bill.

Back and forth. Back and forth. Ha, ha.

Neither of us wanted the damn thing. We hid it everywhere. Once, she found it in her underwear drawer at her house. That excited and bothered her.

Pretty sneaky, she said.

At the same time this was happening, I finished learning Spanish. I still had Post-it notes everywhere in my apartment. Vocab words stuck everywhere.

I had wanted to become a flight attendant—bouncing over the ocean, digging my toes back into solid land—and the airline said Spanish would help.

Nope.

Look at you, they said to me during an interview, you are one huge mofo. You are way too big to go up, they said.

I still had all the Post-it notes, now, stuck all over my place. The Spanish words for trash can—*cubo de basura*. The word for knife—*cuchillo*.

Those are the ones I could not forget.

During that summer, people came over and ate my food and drank my wine and tried to pronounce things off the Post-it notes and even though I hated Spanish now, I corrected them.

Cuchillo, I would say.

Then slower. Cu-chee-YO, not cuch-ILLO.

See the difference? I would say.

Escucha y repita, I told them.

They left angry, my guests. They called me a pompous ass and kicked the sand candles that lighted my walk.

The girl at work and I finally married.

I told her I might crush her one day.

Really? she said.

Really, I said.

I am so large and you are so tiny, so probably it will happen, I told her.

Really? she asked.

.....

One night, rolling around naked, we found some coins in our bed.

Who knows about these things?

They could have come from anywhere, far away, so close, pockets. They weren't like a two-dollar bill. You write your name on a two-dollar bill and pay for something and someday when it returns to your wallet you can say—see, see, I told you so.

These were coins, though, coins, maybe ours to begin with and maybe not.

INVENTORY

.....

Our baby swallowed a ninja star and then it swallowed a Bakelite button. It seemed fine. Breathing and everything. We checked. We are fine parents.

We weren't too upset about the button, but the ninja star was one of my husband's favorites, really light and made from this tungsten polymer that was said to be "space age." He used it in the league that he was in on Thursdays nights.

"I'll never ever find another one like that again," he told me privately.

The same thing happened with our toenail clippers.

One night, I found the baby (who knows how babies do this) standing on top of our bathroom sink, rifling through the medicine cabinet.

"The nail clippers are gone," my husband told me after taking stock. "They were right here on this shelf and now they are not."

"Maybe you left them downstairs," I offered. "Maybe you're mistaken. Maybe you left them somewhere where you forgot. Maybe you were the one."

My husband had just gotten out of bed and his hair was all matted down. It looked like when a helicopter comes down suddenly in high grass, pushed out in spots, flattened down in others.

"Whose side are you on here?" he asked me.

"No one's," I told him. "And everyone's."

Soon, my husband and the baby were eyeing each other in a manner I did not like. You see it all the time nowadays, this raising of eyebrows, a puffing out of chests, hands flexing from open to closed.

One night, my husband searched the baby's bassinet.

"This is a random search," he told the baby. "It could occur at any time. That's what random means, okay?"

The baby took its revenge for the search by swallowing my husband's wristwatch.

"It's on," my husband told our marriage counselor. "That was an heirloom. Handed down from generation to generation. Game fucking on."

"Maybe the baby will pass all this stuff," I offered.

Pass it? That was one thing we knew the baby would NOT do. Things disappeared inside this baby, pellets of rock salt, packs of Post-it notes, diamond solitaire necklaces, whatever. Gone. Finito. Seeya.

Sometimes I put my head right up to the baby's stomach, my ears to its stomach skin, and listened to its innards to see if I heard something moving along.

Passing these things?

"Good one," my husband said. "Hardy-har."

Finally, I started leaving things out for the baby to swallow. A puzzle piece with no matching puzzle. A broken half of a letter opener. A combination lock to which we'd forgotten the combination.

I put these things in plain view.

I left out sheets of paper, too. Words written on them in big black marker. Words like "Crying Over Nothing." Words like "Taking All This For Granted."

I motioned to the baby.

"Here," I said.

I gave the baby one of those sudden *hey, hey over here* moves you give with your hands when you think someone can help.

One morning, I woke up to find my hand duct taped to my husband's hand, this big silver cocoon running up to both our elbows like a shiny cast.

I knew right away.

No note, no word of thanks, not one iota of goodwill for the time that we'd put in. Just the duct tape around our arms.

"Call everyone we know," I said to my husband.

He picked up the phone in his free hand, held it out to me. With my free hand, I dialed. After I punched in the numbers, he held the phone up to his ear.

"Hello," he said to our people, "the baby's gone."

"Not our fault," I called from the background.

"Not our fault," he repeated.

Later that night, after we'd broken the news to everyone, we got up and walked around the house. Looked at what was left.

"Garlic press," we said. "Recordable DVD. Alarm clock."

We touched these things, ran our free hands over them.

After a while, we found a notebook.

This was a lucky thing.

In it, we started to take inventory.

All it boiled down to was this: one person telling the other one what they saw, then the other person, the one with the pen and the free hand, writing it all down.

THE DOJO

.....

I stole my yoga teacher Michelle's wallet because she was stupid enough to leave it sticking out of her purse for me to steal and because I think there are hard lessons about the real world besides remembering to inhale and exhale that can be taught inside the dojo or whatever the fuck they call it. There was two hundred dollars and a bus card in her wallet and the next day I rode the bus back to the dojo for free and used her cash to buy an unlimited monthly yoga pass.

"I didn't think you liked coming here," Michelle said to me. "You kept saying you hated it."

The real reason I kept coming back here was because Evelyn, a pretty brunette who I semi-stalked, occasionally came here to decompress from me semi-stalking her. Evelyn had recently changed apartments and phone numbers and the yoga dojo was now my best chance to locate her.

"No way," I told Michelle. "It's the exact opposite. I love coming here."

.....

I'd stolen a pair of light blue panties from Evelyn's dresser and now whenever I went to yoga I carried these panties in my pocket to help me achieve Zen or whatever it was called. Sometimes I pulled them out to wipe the sweat from my forehead. The panties were silky and they didn't do much to sop up perspiration, but I used them anyway. I was waiting for Evelyn to show up and see me wiping my brow with them. I thought she might get a real kick out of that.

After class that night, Michelle was outside, smoking.

"Are you supposed to be doing that?" I asked. "Isn't that against your teachings or something?"

Michelle had extremely long arms. When her hand was at her side it took her forever to get her cigarette up to her mouth.

"I was really off my game tonight," she said. "I totally fucked up the tilted crane."

She flicked her cigarette onto the sidewalk and then immediately lit another one.

"Are you okay?" I asked.

"Really bad week," she said.

The next day Michelle was not at class.

"Where's Michelle?" I asked the sub.

"She called in sick," the woman said.

Since I had her wallet, I knew where Michelle's apartment was. After class, with the last of her money, I bought her a bouquet of tulips.

"How did you know where I lived?" she asked me when she answered the door.

"That's not important," I said, holding out the flowers.

I had given women presents before, but usually they were presents that they did not appreciate. This present, though, something felt different. It was like these flowers had pulled our two worlds into alignment, and now she and I were cosmically even or whatever it is people say when something like this happens.

Michelle wrapped her long arms around my neck and pulled me in tight. "This was so sweet of you," she said.

"Really," I whispered into her pretty ear, "it was nothing."

My First Wife

.....

It was our anniversary and we celebrated with a cupcake and a single candle. I'd found some walkie-talkies in the dumpster and you ran outside to see if they worked. I sat at the kitchen table and listened as you told me that you thought you heard "truckers in between the static of us."

The next year, I brought you a rock polisher I'd found at a garage sale. I know, I know, not very romantic. Still, you once had told me that you adored polished agates like the ones you saw in the bins at the curiosity shoppes. You told me that you liked the idea of holding a piece of rough earth in your hand and then hours later seeing it buffed it to a high shine.

I remember that you read the instructions for the rock polisher to me out loud. It was hot and we were sitting on that shit-brown couch of ours that we'd found on the curb and huffed the 14 blocks home. As you read, your voice was full and confident, like you were announcing a fire sale on tires or carpet. Be prepared for the constant sound of rolling rocks, you announced. Be prepared for the constant noise.

I laughed it off—how loud could it really be, I said, how loud?

Only when we started it up did we know. It was incredible, that sound. It was like there was an airplane passing right over the top of us, swallowing up everything we said. I kept telling you to switch it off, but you could not even hear me. Everything that came out of my mouth sounded loud and hissing.

Octane

.....

I'm testing pump octane at a Shell station in St. Cloud when a warlock casts a spell over me. He's got a black goatee and his ponytail is pulled back into a green scrunchie. He comes out of the station munching on a fruit pie and then he gives me a smile and a little nod. That's all it takes. I suddenly feel compelled to follow him wherever he goes.

The warlock makes a right turn on the frontage road and so do I. He stops to pick up his dry cleaning and I pull my car right up next to his and wait.

When he comes out of the dry cleaner's, I motion him over. I expect this will be the point where he explains what he has in store for me, sexually or workwise, but instead, he plays it cool.

"Lady," he asks, "Are you following me?"

Truth be told, I do not have time for this. I'm on a strict work schedule. I work for Weights and Measures, drive from gas station to gas station all across our great state. I make sure that no one sells you gas that makes your car shoot blue exhaust or makes your engine knock and ping.

Usually everything checks out, but last week, I caught a guy in Shakopee selling watered-down product.

"Do you understand what this does to an engine?" I asked the man. I shook my testing beaker at him, showed how the water had separated from the gas.

"Can we arrive at a compromise?" the man said as he popped open the cash register and slid a stack of twenties across the counter. "Would this smooth things out?"

I shook my head. I pushed the money back at him. I told the man there was no compromise available. I told him that sometimes you have to own up to the truth and its consequences. I told the man that sometimes a sad heart can suddenly transform back into a wide-lipped chalice and that if you don't hope for that with every fiber of your being, you are a crazy person.

"Are we still talking about octane?" the man asked me.

"We most certainly are," I said.

The warlock peels out from the dry cleaner's and I trail behind him. While I drive, I take a pine tree air freshener and rub it into my cleavage. Because of my job I smell like gas. Some people like this smell, but some people cannot stand it. My dead husband Ronald, rest his soul, loved it.

When Ronald died six months ago, I burned him in the backyard. I didn't say buried, I said burned. It's not legal here either, burning someone in your backyard, but that was what Ronald told me he wanted. I built a huge bonfire and I tied Ronald onto a wood plank like he was a piece of salmon and I pushed the plank onto the fire. Then I sat in a lawn chair and watched him disappear.

The warlock turns into a Renaissance Faire and he parks his car and then he runs inside the gates. I buy a ticket and follow him. I can't find him right away when I get inside, so I purchase a bag of saltwater taffy and then I buy a big leg of turkey. Soon, I see the warlock standing behind a table of silver jewelry. I unbutton another button on my blouse and walk over and stand in front of his table. I wait for him to tell me what he wants me to do.

"I think that there's been some sort of misunderstanding here," he says.

I look at his wares. Spread out before him are gothic snake rings and small ceremonial maces and tiny daggers in little leather sheaths.

"You cast your spell," I tell him. "And now you have to live with that. That's how it works, okay?"

I move to unbutton another button on my blouse, but the warlock grabs my wrists, stops them.

"Hold on now," he says.

The warlock's hands are moist. He reaches down and picks up a ring from his table and he slips it onto my finger. He looks deeply into my eyes.

"This ring," he tells me, "sets you free."

As he says these words, my legs jelly. I grab the table to hold myself up. I feel like maybe this is what a magnet feels like when it has been pulled away from its metal—its strong pull, suddenly separate and distinct.

As I walk back to my car, I weave through the men and women dressed in their Medieval fineries. I walk through the smell of mead and honey and the sounds of simple and joyous laughter.

I find my car in the parking lot and I get in and turn the key. I hear the gas trickle from the fuel line and then I hear that tiny spark, that small bit of combustion deep inside all that metal, the small fire that starts everything into motion.

The Two Malls

.....

There are two shopping malls in my town, expensive and cheap. The expensive one is two stories and has a Sharper Image. The cheap one is low-slung and smells like old chili.

Once, at the cheap mall, I went into the dollar store and watched a man with a missing arm steal a carton of cigarettes by stuffing it into the floppy sleeve of his jacket.

Well done, I wanted to tell him.

The kind of bridge I like best is a cantilever. The kind of sweater I like best is cable knit. A great time to be a whore would have been 1978. You and I might have nothing in common except collecting tiny metal spoons, but those tiny spoons might be enough for us to fall madly in love, okay?

Sometimes at the expensive mall, I buy a cup of soda from the hot dog stand and then balance it on the aluminum railing. I walk away to the other side of the mall and I wait until someone below is about to walk underneath the cup. I hit the railing as hard as I can and the railing vibrates and the cup dumps onto the person below. After I do this I go into the Sharper Image and use the massage tool on my low back. People never get kicked out of places for being too happy.

I saw the man with the missing arm get on the bus a month or so ago. He snuffed his half-smoked cigarette out on a bus shelter and then he tucked it back into the pack very carefully.

"That used to be your arm," I said when he sat down near me.

"What did you say?" he asked me.

"I said that your cigarette used to be your arm."

The man shook his head.

"Everything used to be my arm," he said.

Sometimes at the expensive mall, I don't do the cup thing. Sometimes I just sip my soda and lean over the railing and look down at all the young girls throwing their coins into the fountain. Love is not at all expensive and my arms will be my arms forever. This is what all of them are thinking.

Do Not Touch Me Not Now Not Ever

.....

Last night, Jessup drank 14 Mint Juleps. Then he got out his t-shirt cannon. He dragged a box of t-shirts from the back of his garage and threw them into my car.

"Let's go shoot them at the river barges!" he yelled.

Jessup had just lost his job at the screenprinting place. I was in the midst of a messy divorce. He was wasted. I was too sad to lift a glass up to my lips.

"Remember the goat?" he asked.

In college, Jessup and I had stolen a goat. We snuck it into our dorm room, but its smell was horrible. After an hour we drove it back to its pasture.

"Remember how the goat chewed through all our speaker wire?" he said. "Remember how it kept headbutting my bunk bed?"

I was sick of talking about the goat. I was sick of talking about my ex-wife. I was tired of rehashing all the stupid shit that I'd ever said and done. Unfortunately all of the dumbasses I knew ONLY wanted to discuss these things.

"I won't ever forget that fucking goat," I told Jessup.

We stood on the river bridge and Jessup shot t-shirts at the barges that passed below.

"Are you sure you don't want a try?" he asked.

Lately, instead of sleeping at night, I walked around the city. I walked and walked until my legs cramped up and my bunions burned. Sometimes I called my ex-wife and left rambling voicemails describing the places I ended up. Sometimes I laid down in the middle of the street and counted to a hundred, hoping for a car to fly down the road and slice my body in two.

"I'm totally fine," I told Jessup. "You have your fun."

When Jessup ran out of t-shirts, he shoved his shoe into the cannon. He shot it at a duck, but it splashed down well short of the bird.

"Maybe we should call it a night," I said. "Maybe we've reached the point of diminishing returns here, you know?"

Jessup ignored me, loaded his belt into the cannon. It flapped through the air like he'd thrown a snake. He kept on stripping and shooting. Soon the only thing he was wearing was his watch.

My legs were dead tired, but I still wanted to go on my nightly walk. I still wanted to call my ex-wife and have my call roll directly into her voicemail. I still wanted to lie down on the road and count very, very slowly to infinity.

"Give me your shirt," Jessup begged. "Or your pants. A shoe. C'mon man!"

I shook my head, started to walk away.

"This train is leaving," I told Jessup.

I took a few steps toward my car and then I heard the pop of the t-shirt cannon. Suddenly, there was a searing pain in the back of my thigh. I looked down and saw Jessup's watch sticking out of it.

"Your wife sure did a number on your ass," he said. "I hardly even recognize you anymore."

That was it. I pulled the watch from my leg and then I ran at Jessup. I punched him in the throat and then nailed him in the side of the head. I put him in headlock and held him there.

"Don't stop," he huffed. "Keep going. Let all this shit out already!"

I kept going. I held up my arms and screamed at the night sky.

"Arrrgghhhhgghhh!" I yelled.

My voice bounced off the limestone cliffs of the river and returned to where I stood. It echoed all around me, fierce and timeless.

Guns and Gold

.....

This is glacier country and sometimes stupid people stumble onto valuable shit. Skulls and arrowheads, crude tools, leg bones dragged from god knows where. My father shoves a couple bills across the counter and tells them to bring in anything else they find. When they leave, he calls the natural history museum in Boise. In a couple of hours, a man in a blue car drives down and spreads hundred-dollar bills on the counter like a Japanese fan.

I'm fourteen and these are the two weeks a year I spend with my dad. The first thing he tells me about the pawn business is that most things people hold dear to their hearts are worth little to him. Chipped Elvis plates, broaches passed from mother to daughter, guitars with necks twisted like dead geese—he shakes his head no, no, no.

"Guns and gold," he tells everyone who brings in something that won't sell, "I always buy guns and gold."

.....

One day, a man named Titus pushes a lawn mower through the doors. Yesterday he brought in a weed whip. He was in stocking feet then, but today he has not even bothered with the socks.

"Five bucks," my father says.

"Five bucks is what you say for everything I bring in," Titus whines.

My father thinks I am a pussy because I quit playing hockey; he thinks I am pussy because I don't want to play football in the fall. He thinks he's a great judge of character, thinks he can read people's needs and desires in seconds flat. He only deals with desperate people though. He has forgotten that the only thing you need to know with desperate people is how to simply stand there and wait.

"Five bucks is what it's worth," my father tells Titus. He pops open the till and takes the money and lays it in front of Titus.

Titus stares at it for a couple of seconds. I watch him trying not to grab it, to hold out, to make his feet move toward the door, but then he just cannot help himself. He snatches the money and shuffles out the door.

"Christ," he mutters.

There is a path worn through the grass in the city park, a line of beaten dirt that extends directly from my dad's shop to the liquor store. Sometimes the owner of the liquor store, Sam, stops by and purchases a lot of what my dad buys.

"Your business is our business," Sam tells him. "We're open because you are open."

I am cleaning the jewelry cases with Windex. I take out a flat of rings and I set them on top of the counter. I spray the inside of the underside of the glass and then I reach my arm deep inside and wipe down the dusty front plate.

"That's what is commonly referred to as a symbiotic relationship," I tell them.

"A-symbi-what?" Sam asks.

"Symbiotic," I repeat.

I am just making conversation, but my father grabs onto my shoulder and pushes me toward the front door.

"The sidewalk needs sweeping," he tells me. "Now."

Two days before I leave to go back home, my father drives me up into the lesser Tetons. He tells me we are going to hunt for agates but then he stops the van and tells me to get the fuck out. I stand on the side of the road and he hands me a canteen of water and bag of dry cereal. He pulls the compass off his dashboard of his van and drops it into my palm.

"Due East," my father says. "Walk due East and you'll be just fine."

I stare at the compass' black abyss. I wait for it to stop moving, to find East. Then I start walking. After about five minutes a man in a brown station wagon pulls over. There's a big dog sleeping in the back seat.

"Did someone leave you out here?" he asks.

"Yep," I say. "My dad."

The man tells me to get in and I do. Then he floors it. After about twenty minutes, he passes by my father's van.

"That was him," I say.

"My dad did this same shit to me," the man says. "And you would have probably done it to your son. But now we've broken the cycle, haven't we? Right?"

"Sure," I tell him.

The man drops me off in front of the pawn shop, wishes me good luck and shakes my hand goodbye. I sit down on the curb and wait for my father to return. I stare out at the mountains. There is a lake in front of them and they are reflected upside down in the water.

In a few minutes, my father drives up. I can tell that he is shocked that I am sitting here, but he hides it well enough. He's owned a pawn shop far too long to let any sort of surprise or excitement flash across his face.

"How'd you get back?" my father asks.

I stand and walk toward the shop.

"I asked you a question," he says.

I do not say anything. Instead, I push his compass back into his hand and walk inside.

Let him wonder how I got here, I think. Let him watch the world rotate and list and bob. Let him wait until the compass slowly settles on what things are where and what things are not.

Shoo, Shoo

.....

Shoo, shoo, my wife said, but those were not the words. Quite obviously those were not the words. We might as well have thrown a bottle of Jack and a dime bag of skunk weed down from our bedroom window and said, hunker down fellas, stay awhile. These were jazz musicians and my wife had said shoo.

Earlier that day, we'd gotten the test results. It ended up being both of our faults. Her eggs were bad and my sperm were lazy. We sat in the parking lot of the clinic for about an hour after our appointment, in that car of ours that started with a screwdriver and stopped by pulling up on the emergency brake. I paged through a glossy pamphlet that made adoption look cool and fun.

"I was ready to blame you and then *pretend* I wasn't blaming you," she said. "I was ready to blame myself and then not believe you when you said it wasn't my fault."

"Exactly," I told her.

"I really don't know what to do now," she told me.

"Totally," I said.

I'd already called the cops. I'd already held the phone out the window and let the police dispatcher listen to the racket below, the joshing and stumbling and bellowing and knee slapping and the occasional horn bleat and rim shot.

"In my neighborhood, noise like that would be welcome," the dispatcher told me. "I'd love to hear some noise like that sometime."

I hung up the phone and kneaded my wife's shoulders, pushing against the braids of her back muscle until I found bone.

"Maybe we could have a miracle baby," I offered. "One of those against all odds babies that never should have happened. Everyone else has them," I said. "Why not us?"

After I said this, my wife got up and put on her robe. I watched as she began to drag our dresser across the bedroom floor. It was huge, this dresser, claw-footed, an heirloom, her grandmother's and her grandmother's grandmother before that.

"What are you doing?" I asked.

I watched as she lifted the dresser on the window sill and then pushed it out the window. There was a loud crash, then a clattering of instruments, then voices yelling out below. My wife walked across the room and lifted up a bedside table and then tossed that out as well.

The musicians had run off by then, gone to wherever it is jazz musicians go when people get tired of their shenanigans, but my wife kept on—the good silverware, the coffee pot, those super-sharp knives.

I got up and went into the bathroom. I took wet toilet paper and stuffed it into my ears. I laid down inside our tub and shut my eyes and listened to my heart beating all around me.

Vessels

.....

A man recently brought me this metal briefcase. He set it down on the bar near where I sat. Somehow he knew where to find me. He started calling me by my given name, Ronald. It was getting cold outside, but he was really sweating, this man, these little rivers of water running down his forehead.

"This was your father's," he said pushing the case toward me. "I worked with him. I think he'd want you to have it."

I hadn't talked to my father in a long while. Years now. My mother had died a long time ago. Last I heard my father was traveling around Ohio selling aluminum siding.

I picked up the metal case. I could tell the handle on it had melted a little, but then had cooled down. It had this drippy plastic look that you see sometimes when things get too hot.

"There was a fire," the man told me. "At his motel."

The man proceeded to tell me that someone had fallen asleep smoking in a roadside motel that my father was staying in. This was outside Akron, he said. His briefcase was the only thing left over from his room. It was one of the only things out of the entire place that had made it, he said. The man told me he was driving through here on business, so he thought he'd bring it along and give it to me.

"Heat like that—everything usually melts," he told me. He pointed at the briefcase. "This made it through, though."

The man looked really thirsty, so I got Geno the bartender to put down his tattoo magazine and bring us some drinks.

"Are you okay?" I asked the man. With all the sweat, he wasn't looking so healthy.

"I need to show you something," he said.

We walked outside to his car and he popped open the trunk. My eyes took a second to focus, but when they did, I couldn't believe what I saw—there were three little girls in there, sleeping. There was a bigger one and then the other two got progressively smaller, like Russian stacking dolls.

"They're still my kids," he told me. "Even if their mother doesn't think so."

I kept on looking in that trunk. It was huge! The kids had pillows and blankets and they looked really comfortable. I noticed that the man had drilled some holes in the trunk for ventilation. I wondered why I hadn't thought of doing something like this to a car.

"Wow," I told him.

He shut his trunk gently and we walked back into the bar. He was sweating less now, had calmed down some. After a bit, he pointed at my father's briefcase.

"Aren't you going to look at what's inside?" he asked.

I hadn't thought of it, I hadn't even thought there was anything important inside there, but I popped the latch on it the case and slid it open. I started looking through the stuff in there, what was left of my father. There were some invoices written out in my father's hand, a pack of cigarettes, some siding brochures.

"I was hoping for gold bricks," I said. "But no such luck."

The man and I sat there silently watching the football game on TV for a few minutes. Then he stood up to go.

"Hey," I said. "Can I see them one last time?"

He nodded and we walked out to his car and he opened the trunk. The girls were still in there, all three of them, safe and asleep, same as before.

"Great," I told him. "Thank you for doing that."

The man slowly closed the trunk and we shook hands. Then he got in his car and drove off down the street. After a little bit, he put on his blinker, turned the corner and disappeared.

About the Author

.....

John Jodzio is a winner of the Loft-McKnight Fellowship. His stories have appeared in *One Story*, *Barrelhouse*, *Opium*, *The Florida Review*, and various other places in print and online. A collection of his short stories, *If You Lived Here You'd Already Be Home*, was recently published by Replacement Press. He lives in Minneapolis. Find out more at www.johnjodzio.net.

Paper and Tassels

:: *by Mary Miller* ::

Acknowledgments

"Love" *Frigg*
"Angel" *Vestal Review*
"Open" *Quick Fiction*
"Autobiographies of the Other Sister" *Pank* online
"Diagnosis" *Hobart* online
"A Detached Observer" *Storyglossia*
"Destiny" *Quick Fiction*
"Paper and Tassels" *Journal of Truth and Consequence*
"Watermelon" *Night Train*
"Patterns" *The Pedestal*
"Every Day" *Black Clock*
"Misled" *Pank* online
"Girls" *Journal of Truth and Consequence*
"My Old Lady" *Storyglossia*
"Aesthete" *Wigleaf*
"Baby/Hon" *Versal*

Table of Contents

LOVE

.....

She digs her nails into my arm and I let her because this is what she knows of love. You don't want to hurt me, do you? I ask and she nods her head yes. She shows me the scars on her legs, gifts from her daddy. Little nicks of missing skin, tiny craters. I let her leave her marks. I'm the adult. She's the child. But both of us want to see blood. She presses not quite hard enough to break the skin and stops, leaving crescents up and down my arm. It's not nice, I say. Is that nice, to hurt me? Yes, she says. It's nice. But then she runs her hand up and down, smoothing out the dents, trying to make them go away.

Angel

.....

Reggie stays up all night to watch me sleep. I know because I catch him, his eyes glowing in the dark. He watches me because I won't be around for long. He watches me because I'm the consistency of vapor.

At the pool, he's wearing a baseball cap pulled low over wet eyes, drinking vodka from a Coke can so he can take it up to the architecture building later and get drunk while he works.

"Jesus, I love you," he says, lying on the concrete with his feet in the water. It's late. I want to go home and go to sleep but I feel obligated to pretend I care because I've been sleeping with him, and in his world, girls are supposed to care about the men they let enter them.

"It's good to love Jesus," I say.

"You're a bitch."

He doesn't see me wave goodbye. I climb the stairs to my apartment taking two at a time. On the balcony, I look down and he's still lying there churning the water so I pick up someone's pack of cigarettes from the table and light one, smoke it past the camel. Then I go inside and sit on the stiff couch that came with the place.

My roommate Annie says, "You know he was over here earlier. I fixed him a sandwich."

"Don't fix him any more sandwiches."

"He was hungry."

"Everyone's hungry," I say. "We can't feed them all."

I go to my room and shut the door and lock it because my other roommate brings home strange men. The last one read my palm and said I would die soon.

I met Reggie at a party the first week of school. I was there with my roommate Hadley, the one who brings home strange men. She said, "That guy is burning a hole in you," and it had been a long time since someone burned a hole in me. I went home with him that night. His bed was a mattress on the floor and there were clothes and towels everywhere. His sheets smelled like oranges. I held his penis in my hand like a thick rope of sausage. "I don't think it will fit anywhere," I said. "That's okay," he said. He didn't say, "Let's try." He didn't say, "It will," or explain that the vagina was designed to stretch to accommodate a baby's head. I woke up around four because I had to use the bathroom and he was propped up on one elbow looking at me with those huge purplish-white love eyes.

"You're an angel," he said.

"I don't like that kind of talk."

"But you are. You should believe it."

And every night we've spent together since has been the same: the nocturnal staring, the angel talk, me peeing and then having trouble going back to sleep because I can feel his eyes struggling to memorize my face before it's gone.

Open

.....

See him rounding the corner in the midday heat, wearing the nice lined pants he used to work in, cut off at the knee. Swim over to the side of the pool, rest your arms on the concrete, and ask where he's going.

The library, he says, his man-purse on.

Offer him the car, by which you mean your car, but don't call it your car because he doesn't have one and you don't want to keep pointing out all the things he doesn't have, which is nearly everything.

I can walk, he says. Kick off. Swim breaststroke while a hairy, burning man reads a paperback. It is just the two of you, fenced in. Look to see if he's looking, find he isn't. Be disappointed. Switch to butterfly. Almost drown: still nothing. Hold on to the side of the pool for a bit to catch your breath. Remind yourself that even if this man wanted you, you would not want him. Then tell yourself it's not the point.

Climb out and walk down the hill to your apartment.

Make a sandwich, a list, a pan of brownies: distract yourself. Give up. Call him. Ask when he'll be home, knowing that with this call you are forfeiting, and that he has won.

Sometime within the next four hours, he says.

Be sure to leave yourself an open window, you say, and throw the phone across the room. Lie down on the couch, letting your hair soak the pillow. The couch isn't paid for but it is yours enough to ruin. Roll down your swimsuit and look at the bruises on your breasts. Touch one; press down. Touch another; press. Find they only look like they hurt.

Think about men, how you don't like it when they are too old or too new.

Think about the man's tongue, which spends a lot of time outside his mouth, and how he insults you in ways so small you feel badly for pointing them out.

Remember that there are stories in simple things, or ways to make simple things complex. Close your eyes: wait. Open them. Stare at the black spot on the ceiling until it starts to move and call again. Tell him to come home. When he asks for twenty minutes, give them to him.

Autobiographies of the Other Sister

.....

Condo

They were talking about their diseases.

Dating in the Twenty-first Century, one of them said.

I'm never sleeping with anybody ever again, said the other, and the first one didn't disagree. They were sisters. They never touched each other but they could talk openly now, after a decade of not talking openly because they had each expected the other to be better than themselves. For a long time, they were disappointed.

One of them helped the other clean her condo. The one who lived in the condo showed the other one how dirty certain things were, like her pillowcase. This is what my life is, she was saying. They hung clothes until the couch was visible; they Swiffered and scrubbed. Then they went out to lunch, to a sports bar with plans of getting drunk. One of them smoked and looked out the window while the other watched the tall, probably gay bartender and sang along to muzak.

Finally, their eyes settled on each other.

It's so good to see you, one of them said.

You say that every time, said the other. Then they went back to what they were doing. It was the end of February and there weren't any sports to speak of, only coaches imagining seasons that had not yet begun.

Pretty

She hadn't known anyone in her building until the night of a storm when a bunch of them ended up in the stairwell, drinking. Now she knew the man who lived below her.

She was doing her kickboxing video, the same one she always did. The man who lived below her sent a text message: Impressive jump rope. She texted him back and he texted her and then the discourse, and her workout, was over. Later, her sister brought groceries, bread and milk and bananas. They looked at Victoria's Secret catalogues, picking out swimsuits. One of them liked the busy ones and the other liked the plain ones, solid colors with no cut-outs to leave stars or hearts or phalluses on her body.

I weigh a hundred and fourteen pounds now, one of them said.

That's awesome, said the other, flicking the skin on her sister's upper arm.

The one who only weighed a hundred and fourteen pounds used to weigh much more. At night she'd lie in bed and feel her bones and hate herself, remembering the times she had hit on men when she hadn't known she was fat.

They were dark-haired and equally pretty. They had moles on opposite sides of their faces like looking in a mirror.

Business

She called her sister to ask whether she had kept her appointment to have her computer fixed. She hadn't. But she had done other things on her list: called people who were going to call her back, scheduled other appointments to miss. Neither of them had a husband to take care of such things. One of them couldn't keep a man and the other couldn't stay kept.

What happened was I got drunk, said the one who hadn't kept her appointment.

It's just now dark, said the other.

Usually I lay in bed and wait for whatever I was supposed to be doing to be over, but Cat called.

The other dropped her phone on the pavement and the conversation got cut off and then they were calling each other at the same time so they kept getting sent to voicemail.

Finally, they reconnected.

I dropped my phone, said the first one.

I thought it was me, said the second. My phone never works at Cat's house.

The first one didn't know who Cat was, but she could hear her in the background, cackling.

Different

They were at a coffee shop near the college. It was Monday and Fido's was full of notebooks and laptops. They were past all that. They ordered coffee and muffins and sat at the only empty table. One sister took the good seat and the other had a view of the wall.

It's good people watching, the one with the good seat said.

Not so much for me, said the other.

The one with the good seat turned around and looked at the red slab of wall, the ugly paintings for sale. One of them was the oldest and the other was the baby and they held the same opinion of each other: spoiled; everything she ever wanted.

They took pinches off each other's muffins and sipped each other's coffee to determine whose was better, the winner obvious. They had their elbows on the table, fingers dusting off bits of muffin. They weren't like other girls, they didn't think.

Diagnosis

.....

Her heart swells like someone turned a faucet on. It is enormous. A fast-moving cloud of blackbirds dissipates into the trees. Or are they bats? They're at the zoo. It is the same as the bowling alley or the skating rink only there are animals. The sky looks like snow. The thirty-year-old woman doesn't know what the twenty-two-year-old girl was like. She only knows this: the girl spent a lot of time in the mirror but she never saw herself. The boy asks if she wants a Coke, she says she doesn't, he gets one and she drinks most of it. They watch a couple of rhinos on a mound of dirt, just standing there. It looks boring, she says. It must be boring to be a rhinoceros. He agrees. She says the same thing about the spider monkeys and the elephants and the giraffes and he agrees, but at the manatees he says: you're boring. They marry, live like old people.

A Detached Observer

.....

I get off work early and go over to his house. He's out back in the dark with a pair of binoculars in his lap.

"Stars pulse," he says. "Planets don't. That's how you can tell them apart."

From down here everything seems to pulse but I don't say that. He has recently discovered how far away the sun is, how fucking far away, or maybe he knew all along but didn't care before.

"Let's swim," he says.

We strip off our clothes, bound down the steps and into the pool. I grab onto the diving board and pull myself up, but it doesn't matter that I'm beautiful, doesn't change the way he sees me.

"Nice tits," he says.

"I'd fuck me," I say.

Then I do flips until I'm dizzy. I untuck myself and float on my back while the stars crawl across the sky and the world straightens itself back out. He gets out of the pool, jogs up the steps and into the house.

He stays gone for a few minutes, plenty of time to make a phone call, for instance, and returns with a pint of whiskey.

"You try too hard," he says, sitting on the steps in the shallow end, his penis bobbing in the water like a cork. He takes a hard pull as if this distance is my fault. I don't say anything because I can't think of any way to win this conversation and there is certainly no way for me to win him, so I swim butterfly from one end of the pool to the other, displacing as much water as I can, while he watches me.

Destiny

.....

When I woke up, I couldn't remember what we'd fought about, just that we'd fought.

Last night I'd gotten drunk because we'd gone to a bar. I tried to stay out of bars. I wasn't good at pacing myself in situations where the whole point was to drink as much as possible while acting sober. I'd get drunk and black out just to remind myself what a hangover felt like.

I scooted over and pressed my body to his, but it was a bad spot, the middle of the futon, the metal rod intersecting. The locks on the windows were broken; you had to jiggle the handle on the toilet to get it to stop running; the carpet was old and gathery. I'd left my husband six months earlier. I knew this poverty was temporary but I couldn't see any way around it. If I didn't have a man taking care of me, I'd be poor. Even if I had a good job and made a lot of money.

"What were we fighting about last night?" I asked him.

"We weren't fighting," he said. His idea of fighting was knockdown-dragout. His ex-girlfriend had been a combative alcoholic, had given him black eyes. I'd bring her up because he still loved her. We'd be eating the buffet at Shoney's and I'd ask about the time she overdosed on Adderall, or what she usually made him for breakfast, and he'd talk about her for two plates and I'd be mad.

"I remember fighting about something," I said.

"You said you hated me."

"That was it. I got in trouble."

"You didn't get in trouble. I just don't like it when you say you hate me. You have to be careful when you say things like that—it's like when you say you want to break up. If you say it enough, it'll happen."

"Don't tell me, 'you make your own destiny,'" I said. "I hate it when you tell me that."

"Well, you do."

He went to the bathroom. Then he got back in bed and we listened to the toilet run.

"You have to jiggle the handle," I said.

"It'll stop," he said, and then it did. He was making his own destiny.

"You know I don't hate you, baby," I said.

"I know, baby."

He liked it when I called him baby, liked it so much I'd become baby, too.

We stared into each other's eyes. His eyeballs seemed smaller than normal. They had starbursts in the center like doll eyes and I could see that he loved me. I could accept his love or not. I had trouble making the simplest decisions but we were the same: we'd both walk into a store and point, bring home the first thing we saw.

"I love you," I said.

"I love you, too," he said.

And then we attempted to quantify our love, but his million was equal to my billion-trillion-times-infinity, and the space between his arms as empty as the space between my fingers.

Paper and Tassels

.....

File his stories in your head: Homosexual Experience, Threesomes, Prostitution, Asian Girls. Mostly he fucked people over, which you like because he is in love with you. He will not fuck you over, you tell yourself. At some point he cries and says you are his dream girl. You have no stories to tell. You can count the number of men you've had on one hand, none of them any good. He sends you pictures. He is in the bathroom. He is outside. He is in the kitchen. There is a tea kettle, a window, a cloud. There is a hanging lamp made of paper and tassels.

Watermelon

.....

Mr. Fuller was the new choir teacher. He had a round face and a love of boys. Before we sang, he had us lie on our backs and breathe in the icy waters. Feel the waves lick your neck, he'd say, the sting of peppermint in the back of your throat. Your boat's collapsed and you didn't think you'd need a life preserver. Feel the pressure build. It builds and builds, like when you love someone so much your heart could burst, *your heart could fucking burst* under the weight of it.

After he drowned us, he'd make us form a train and rub each other's shoulders. This went on for months and nobody saying anything.

Mr. Fuller invited the more troubled boys over to his house, got them out of situations he called pickles, grilled burgers.

I went over there with a boy and watched him worry a knife into his foot while Mr. Fuller was inside slicing tomatoes. We were Indian-style on a rotting deck. A long way to fall, I said. He wasn't the kind of boy who held your hand, which was why I liked him, but still I wanted him to reach over and take it. Instead, he unfurled my palm and put the knife in it. Don't give it back to me, he said, no matter what I tell you don't give it back.

He lifted his t-shirt to show me the swastika carved into his chest. Small and red, it fell in the same spot as the angel on my necklace.

Mr. Fuller led us down the stairs to a square of concrete. He pulled a couple of chairs off a stack and nodded, so we sat while he flipped meat.

He talked to the boy without the obvious questions of school and home. I wanted to talk to the boy like that, but mostly I said nothing because I didn't want to say the wrong thing. I scratched my elbow, my ankle, my elbow, my elbow, my ankle. The magazines I read advised me to lightly scratch my appendages to bring the attention back to me, but once you scratch something it starts to itch.

His dog was what my father would call yippy, or yappy. It ran up and down inside the path it had worn. I watched it run and thought about how, when we sang, Mr. Fuller walked slowly, his hands behind his back and his feet going heel-toe, heel-toe, heel-toe. Sometimes he leaned down and put his ear to my lips and half the time I was just staring at the boy and mouthing wa-ter-mel-on, wa-ter-mel-on, wa-ter-mel-on. The other half I was singing my heart out.

Patterns

.....

He has a card table in the laundry room, where he sits. I stand in the doorway. Hi. He takes his glasses off to look at me. The lenses are scratched. They came that way, he accepted them. If there is a single person, anywhere, ever, who has learned from his mistakes then I'd like to meet him, I say. We go to Siam for dinner: Tom kha gai, Pad Thai, fresh spring rolls. He has no money, so I pay. On the way out, he gives the waitress the baby wave, signing the letter A over and over again, which I've repeatedly asked him not to do, but he says, for women, the straight hand in the air feels insufficient, a pitiful offer. Men get the straight hand but women deserve a little something extra. Okay. What about this? he asks, giving me half of a quote unquote. It looks like you're trying to finger somebody, I say. At the place we call home, I ask him to leave. He agrees easily, so I talk him into staying.

Every Day

.....

Every day after school Cary sits on the trunk of his blue-green Honda and you want to ask for a ride but you don't, even though you know he is waiting for you. Instead, you ride home with your brother in your father's Mercury Sable, a car you call the Insurance Man's Car, which is what your father sells. One time on the way to school it started smoking and your brother had to pull over into River Hills Country Club, where you do not belong, to wait for it to cool down.

You and your brother are always late for school but your aunt works in the office and she lets it slide, which exacerbates the problem. You try not to call her Aunt Pammy at school, even though she isn't technically your aunt anymore because your uncle divorced her and moved to San Juan. Your mother says you should still call her Aunt Pammy. At school, you call her nothing. You call her "Hey." Sometimes she winks at you and tucks your hair behind your ear and you think about her three children, your cousins, none of whom you ever liked.

You know exactly how many minutes it takes to get to school. You know you have to leave by 8:12 in order to make first period so every day you sit at the kitchen table, waiting, as 8:12 passes and then 8:15 and there is no way you can make it after 8:15, even if your brother makes every single light. And once you are already late, he doesn't see the point in hurrying. He wants to stop for chicken biscuits or gum or the car is on Empty.

Every day when you get home, you sit in front of the television and eat Lucky Charms or Count Chocula, anything with marshmallows. You pick all the marshmallows out, first in twos and threes and then one at a time, which pisses off your little sister. You watch *Saved by the Bell* and *The Golden Girls*—shows with back-to-back episodes so you don't have to change the channel. Your sister laughs at the television set. You never laugh at it, but sometimes you smile.

Every day your father comes home early and sits in his chair and kicks the family poodle and you ignore the poodle until your father kicks it and then you remember you love it. You remember you love it so much you could crack its ribs with your love. The dog is copper-colored. Her name is Penny. You pick the fleas off her pink belly, cut them in two with your thumbnail.

When your father stops smoking, he still goes outside and stands there. He doesn't stop drinking but your mother says he only drinks when there's a reason. Then she tells you that some people can always think of a reason, which is more than you think your mother should say, but you don't see him drink that much so you don't know what she's talking about. You look for bottles in his closet and under their bed but you don't find any. You find a gun. You pick it up. You do not get the urge to shoot yourself in the head but the idea is there, that you could, which makes you feel better.

You know Cary is waiting for you because he told you so. He tells you things on Friday nights when he's high. You sit in the bushes with him and hide behind walls because your friends are always wondering where you are. Your friends are always saying, come on. Your friends are always saying, let's go, because there is always the idea of something better.

You think, there is plenty of time. You think, soon. It's only September. It's only October. It's only January. There is still time. And every day he's still there, waiting, until one day he isn't and you ask where he went, but nobody knows. You ask what happened, but nobody cares because he hadn't been around that long and nobody thought much of him anyway. It seems like no one even noticed him sitting on his car every day after school, waiting for you.

Misled

.....

When you tell Paul you love him, he gives you a sad look and says he doesn't feel the same way. Then he says, "This hurts me more than it hurts you," and he sits up and slips his jeans on. You watch while he collects the wad of bills and coins from your nightstand. You watch him walk out the door and get in his car, hoping to feel something.

You want to listen to music while you take a bath but your roommate is asleep and there's a boy with her. His name is Timmy and he's uncircumcised. She tells you about penises because you've only seen a handful and they were all the same size and shape and she wants you to know that you've been misled.

Paul calls a week later and says he's been thinking about you.

"Me too," you say, though you only thought about thinking about him, but then found yourself thinking about something else, like this boy you met at Rick's Café who taught you how to throw darts and stuck his tongue in your ear. This boy is with you now. He stands behind you with a pair of scissors and a comb because the world you live in has a high turnover rate, like the chain restaurant along the highway where you wait tables for extra money. People just stop showing up. New people are hired on the spot.

Paul hears your new boyfriend ask a question and says, "Who's that?" and you tell him your new boyfriend. He asks what he's doing and you tell him he is cutting your hair.

"You just let some guy you don't know cut your hair?"

"Yes," you say, and he calls you a whore and hangs up with his decision not to love you confirmed.

Your new boyfriend has never cut hair before.

"How much do you want me to take off again?" he asks, and he shows you some of your hair, still attached, between his index and middle fingers. You tell him a little more than that.

"What if I mess it up?"

"It's wavy so you won't be able to tell. And you don't know me well enough to harbor the kind of resentment it would take to fuck it up on purpose," you say, impressed with how smart you sound. "I cut my ex-boyfriend's hair once. I fucked it all up and he had to get a regular boy haircut and he cried."

"You're not a very nice person," he says.

You don't like your new boyfriend very much. He dresses up like an Indian and goes to powwows. He's skinny but his stomach is fat.

Your roommate stands in the door with her backpack over her

shoulder. She calls you chica, tells you she wants to go to Mexico Tipico for lunch.

"Ask me again in ten minutes," you say.

Your new boyfriend has already told you he doesn't like her. Your roommate has already asked about the size of his penis.

You don't go to Mexico Tipico because you're in bed with your new boyfriend. You start at one side of his wiry unibrow and make your way to the other like you're reading a book. You've missed your Architecture Appreciation class, which is harder than it sounds. You should have taken Music Appreciation or Art Appreciation but you heard Architecture Appreciation was easier. Regardless, you have missed it and you will have to borrow the notes from someone who won't want to lend them to you.

Your new boyfriend is proud of the haircut he gave you. He combs your hair back from your face with his fingers and you close your eyes and think about Paul, how he is probably still holding his phone, how you could call him up and maybe he would come over and do the exact same thing this boy is doing to you now.

Girls

.....

He shows you his drawings, sketchbooks full of naked women. Women who were live at some point, who let him draw them before they became a story he would recount to you. How one day you will be a story he will recount to someone else. You picture him high and biking through the streets of San Francisco. You think you might have loved him then. He points to one drawing, a bar scene, and says, so I'm sitting in this bar in South Korea, watching a group of people who thought they were coming upon the end of the world. They had given all their possessions to a charlatan, and so, when the end didn't come, became very angry. He mimics tearing apart your apartment, holding a lamp over his head before setting it back down, knocking over a chair and then righting it. You like this story, but you want to hear about the Japanese girl again. You want to hear about every girl who ever loved him, hoping that all of them, put together, might somehow convince you.

My Old Lady

.....

Denis called his fiancée my old lady. Growing up, his mother dated bikers.

Denis' fiancée was in Panama City with her girlfriends, in celebration of her upcoming nuptials, while the two of us were in his bed, landlocked and naked.

She cooks and she cleans and she's got this ass, he said, showing me the shape of it with his hands, that's got just the right amount of jiggle. And she's moving up in the world. Not standing still like the rest of us.

Maybe I should do her, I said, to be polite.

My old lady even irons my underwear. And she never burns anything. He said this last part slowly, chewing up every syllable before spitting it back out. You'd like her, he said, a hand between my breasts, and then he lifted the larger one to his mouth. He did this thing with his tongue that felt nice, a thing I did not remember. I laid my head on her pillow and shut my eyes.

I'd never ironed his underwear, or folded them, and I burned everything. Years ago, we lived together in an old house full of old things. Our television had no remote and our stove had no timer, and for some reason it never occurred to me to buy them. He used to like his food burnt. He used to like me, back when my ass had just the right amount of jiggle, back when I was his old lady.

You like that? he said. Old dog's learned some new tricks.

I was moaning. It had been a long time.

Yeah, I said. Mama likes, which was an old trick, bringing his mother into it.

He got on top of me again, said he was gonna turn me out. I turned my face into her pillow. It smelled like sunshine, like it had been dried on a Greek island. I had never been anywhere, but I kept an atlas under my bed, memorized facts I did not need to know.

I wrapped my legs around his middle and squeezed.

Mama likes it when you slap her, I said, and his eyes narrowed like he didn't remember Mama liking that but he reared back and did it anyway. My eyes leaked into her pillow. Then it hit me: the pillowcase had been washed in Gain. When he finished, he pulled out and said Daddy didn't really like that, and I said Mama didn't really like it either, she just wanted to see what it felt like.

Aesthete

.....

I went to a wedding reception at the house of a man who painted with his ass. The largest of these paintings was in his foyer. People stood around it and said, "That's his ass," because you couldn't tell it was his ass until someone pointed it out. I stood with them. I wore a black and purple check skirt, a belt cinched tight around my waist. People were surprised by the size of it.

After, a few of us went out.

I rode in the backseat with a boy I knew from school. He hadn't thought of me before but now he had his hand on my thigh, pinching at my pantyhose. I suspected he was gay. He only paid attention to the most beautiful girls, as if he could only comment on them aesthetically. His hand went up and down. It started a fire. I raised my ass and took my pantyhose off and stuffed them into the clutch my mother let me borrow. It was empty except for a twenty-dollar bill, a tube of lipstick, and a bottle of clear nail polish for runs. She was teaching me how to be a lady. I was supposed to have already learned. The boy in the driver's seat was looking at me in the rearview mirror, alarmed. My brother was in the passenger seat smoking his silver cigarette, not offering it around like he normally did. The boy I suspected was a homosexual said I needed to shave.

We parked and got out. I went straight for the bathroom and hovered over the bowl while I read the words I knew by heart. The sink was water-stained, the mirror cracked down the middle. I reapplied lipstick. When I came out, the boy from the driver's seat was waiting with a can of beer. He was so tall his body had begun to curve back around. People were always asking how tall he was. I was short, but no one ever asked exactly how.

"Thank you," I said, and I stood there for a minute while he tried to open me up and then I went and sat down with the homosexual. I let him run his hand up my skirt. Touch my panties. The ceiling began to leak, the water accumulating on the table. I lit a cigarette and smoked it while watching the drops swell and swell until they could no longer contain themselves.

Baby/Hon

.....

*Already he is baby/*and I am hon/and he's in my bed/with the patch on his shoulder/shaking/because he hasn't been to the doctor to get his Klonopin yet/and he presses his lips/to my forehead/for a long time/too long to be a kiss/and says I am very pretty and very kind/and I know he doesn't mean kind/like he could never love me/so I don't tell him I'm not/I have already told him this before/when I wasn't sure/what he meant/and he said he wasn't kind either/and already his hand is on my ass/and his mouth on my nipple/without asking/so I turn on the lamp/for him to read me a story/from his book/the one with the planet on the cover and the floating spoons/and he flips to the back/to show me the picture of him/blowing up a balloon at his daughter's birthday party/a cone hat on his head/presents/the photo crooked like the taker was drunk/and the first sentence of his bio/says he's a dishwasher/even though he was teaching at a community college then/because his stories are full of poor people/and he'll always be one of them/and he asks if I want funny or sad/and I say sad/and he reads me a story I can't follow/because I'm reading along with him/and too much is scratched out/all of the words/he has had time to decide were wrong.

About the Author

.....

Mary Miller is the author of a story collection, *Big World* (Short Flight/ Long Drive), and a chapbook, *Less Shiny* (Magic Helicopter Press). Her stories have appeared in *McSweeney's Quarterly, Ninth Letter, American Short Fiction, Mississippi Review,* and *Oxford American,* and have been anthologized in *New Stories from the South 2008* and *Dzanc's Best of the Web 2010*. She lives in Austin, where she is a Michener Fellow at the University of Texas.

Dear Mother Monster, Dear Daughter Mistake

::: *Elizabeth J. Colen* :::

Acknowledgments

"Curtains" *Pebble Lake Review*
"The First Time I Lied" *Redivider*
"Rinse and Oxidation" *BLIP*
"Natural Selection" *Juked*
"Shoulder" *Juked*

Table of Contents

I knew an abandoned child who was my mother.
Dead now. And so I know that beauty is a foundling,
A bicycle leaned against a disappearing tree.

—Donald Revell

Until She Comes Looking

Curtains

.....

She wants her mother back and all I can give her is this—over and over. She doesn't want my mouth, wants no kissing anywhere even. Just this. Like this—quiet and rough. Quiet because her stepfather is napping in the bedroom next to ours after having wept all night. We heard him, even fucked through that though neither of us mentioned it or let on that we heard. Her aunts and cousins have been roaming the halls, aimless in grief, tidying things, looking for things to do, things to fix. I worry they will hear us, will come looking for her, will hear this. But if I slow to any softness she pulls on me in a way that lets me know this slowing is unacceptable.

There isn't much in the way of logic I could provide for her. Her mother—her best friend really—dead at fifty from cancer that should have been caught earlier. Spent, she lays her head on my chest. I think of the cells the doctors tried to cut out of her mother here. How incomplete she must have looked without her breasts. How bare. How scarred. How incomplete she must have been when she died, when they burned her. How her ashes have none of this. The nipples missing, the flesh of the breasts. And they cost her too. In life she spent a lot on them, was vain in those ways. What they put into women in the 1960s who didn't have enough of what they wanted, or enough of what men wanted or enough of what women thought they should want—they cost a lot then. And were unsafe. This is where the sickness began. A rupture in the chest the heart had nothing to do with. I feel my chest might burst with the dead heaviness of her on me. Whatever is in her head that makes it feel this way won't ever come out.

I stroke her hair a few times, murmuring, I think motherly almost. This seems to soothe her. I want her to cry. To show she's feeling it, or maybe because I keep crying and it isn't my mother dead. Or maybe I'm jealous she has a mother to mourn, that I wish mine were gone instead so I could forget her. Maybe I want her to cry so I'm not alone in the grief, whatever it is. I let my fingers twine in her hair, to get my hand closer to her head, the heat there maybe, or as though I might tease out her thoughts. I press my fingers into her scalp until she shifts, until she isn't so heavy on my chest. Maybe this is what I wanted. Maybe it wasn't her thoughts at all, not her emotion. But for her to stop being so heavy on me—for me to stop holding so much of her.

There's a knock on the door, a whisper we can't hear—or I can't hear and I assume she can't either. But she says, "I can't" and then "go away" like she's answering something. And I know they are two statements but of course I hear them as one: "I can't go away." And then she says something to me I can't quite make out and then another sound on the door that isn't knocking exactly but maybe a heel catching on the bottom of the door as it turns. And I start to say something. Maybe "I'm sorry," maybe "I love you," maybe "I can't" or "I'm hungry" but all that comes out is "I" before her hands are on my mouth, in my mouth like she's pulling words off my teeth or scratching them off my tongue with her fingers. I start to speak again, around her fingers this time—just two of them in there now pressing down on my tongue and all she says is "no." And then "now, this" and the hand that isn't in my mouth pulls my hand to where she wants it. This is where she always wants it—not in her hair or touching her cheek or back, but here at the center of her. She pulls on me hard, like she wants to be pulled, pushes me like she wants. And her hand slips and I slip, off-balance and jam my chin into her cheek. And I want this to be funny the way it always would have been. "Clumsy lover," she would have said before, "clumsy lover, I love you." But she doesn't say this, just pulls me more and harder, makes me into the right thing, the thing for her. And I start crying again, quietly at first then coughing so it doesn't sound so much like sobs. I don't know if this is for her, or for him in the bedroom next to ours, or for the ones who might be in the hall, or for me, but it's probably for me.

She pushes my head onto her chest. I don't think this is to quiet me or calm me, not really. There's nothing tender in this, nothing nice.

Just to get my tears away from her neck maybe or maybe so I don't hear her say "yes, that's it" like she's embarrassed to be satisfied by anything right now. And I'm memorizing the pattern on the curtains—the camellias and ribbons, the pattern of green leaves on a lighter green background—because I already know her so well, know her body. And I don't want to know any of it right now. Don't want to be in here or in her or inside of me or any of it. I just want to open the curtains and let in some light or I want to hide behind them until she comes looking for me.

The First Time I Lied

.....

The first time I lied it went like this. My brother and I stood outside in front of our father's VW bug. The sky hadn't seen clouds in weeks and the temperature drifted into the one-hundred-and-teens like the neighbor's fat cat sliding off the porch after a meal. The bug's trunk lid stood at attention, held open by a stick my father kept in there. We watched our father wander back and forth from the house to the car and back again, piling our summer things in for a trip to the beach. Where they took us to "the beach" in Kansas I can't remember, though I remember them calling it that.

I noticed a box of laundry detergent wedged toward the back of the trunk, and leaned in to slide it forward while my brother held my feet. I opened the lid and perched the box on the car's lip and inhaled the very smell of our family. My brother leaned in to smell it too, and I tipped it forward to meet his nose. I don't know if I was trying to be helpful or trying to drown him in it.

The box tipped off the lip, not into my brother's face, but down the front of him, over his Doctor Who t-shirt, and into a neat pile on the gravel of the driveway.

The day was windless, still. Had someone told me the afternoon was airless I would have believed it, the weight of the heat itself seemed heavy enough to fill any space.

We looked at the still pile, then spread it around with our feet. Some of the scented specks got stuck between our sweating toes. When our father re-emerged with the beach towels I told him it had snowed.

He reached down and took a handful of it, picked up some gravel too in his hand because of how thinly we had spread it, and held it to his nose. The beach towels brushed against my legs.

"Sure smells good for snow," my father said. He looked me in the eyes. "Should I see how it tastes?"

I didn't blink, stutter or smile. I could hear my brother's sandaled feet shifting in the dirt. I didn't hesitate when I said, "If you want to you should."

My father laughed and let the stuff run through his fingers, brushed his hands together, put the towels in the trunk, went back inside.

Before the screen door even clicked shut I knelt down and grabbed my own fistful. I opened my palm. I was thinking winter. The white stuff practically glowed in the sun. Some grains glistened, sparkled like the magic crystals they were.

I stuck my tongue out—not just the tip of it, but fully flattened it. I ran my tongue across my palm—not to taste detergent, but because I'd forgotten it wasn't snow.

JENNIFER

.....

My mother wanted to name me Jennifer. This was after either the popular girl in her high school, the one boys memorized all the yearbook pages of, or after her best friend in the third grade who moved to Cranbury, New Jersey, and died in a boating accident at age ten.

I was her second choice. She lost the name Jennifer in a game of Gin Rummy to her friend Patty. Both women were seven months pregnant and had had enough of staying off the alcohol. They drank three six packs between them. My mother also lost a pair of shoes and fourteen dollars. She bet the name when there was nothing left. Patty had three children—all boys—and stayed convinced this one would be her girl, her Jennifer, named for a grandmother she'd never met who died of influenza. "Carrie Jean"—the second a family name—was signed on my birth certificate two days before Patty's fourth son Jared was born.

For the whole summer before Jared and I started kindergarten our mothers decided to call both of us Jennifer for the fun of it, for the daughters they never had. To tell us apart when we played together Jared was just "Jennifer" and I was "Jenni," with an "i."

Home Before Dark

.....

The boy I was then stood on a dirt hill miles away from anything. He proclaimed to own it all. Ants climbed his legs and he let them. They died in a V on his jeans, covered in poison stolen from an unlocked shed. Two dirt clods shook boy me into stumbling.

No one owns me.

Rock paper scissors, and only the paper was soft. Only the paper was mine.

Because my name can be spelled wrong, I can be held down too. The protocol of things learned quickly. Face to the mound. They searched for horns in my hair. What a *Jewbie* is, *JAP*, what a *darkie*, a *spic*. What they told us we were, hands to the ground, fist to the back of the neck.

When we were eleven we made slaves of the girls next door. Everything was new then. Shiny like bows in their hair. No one knew how we made them be.

Twenty-four doors slam shut in twenty-four houses. Twenty-four laws. Nightmares untangle slowly, like birds unmaking nests of our hair. Winter meant the devil could know more of us; we could fit three rules on our hands. *Don't show fear. Give away nothing. Home before dark.*

Rinse and Oxidation

.....

I heard a story once about a man who can only tell his wife by her dentist. He schedules the appointment every year; she drives the car. White coat checks incisors and decides it's her, the right wife; they go on for another year, tucked into a ranch-style with no horses, no cowboy anything, just handfuls of brief stairs and long spans of shag carpet.

As a child, head tipped back, I stared at the alphabet or whale on the ceiling, depending on the chair. Red letters mocking the copper taste in my mouth. And for a while my mouth belonged to someone else.

There was machinery and I was lost to its buzzing and mint smell. I was lost to the courtship of gloved fingernails snaking towards the back of my throat.

Questions with no answers.

Gloved fist shaking in front of her face.

When I was five, mother monster stopped holding my hand. She was like this in everything. At eight, church became a choice and we never heard bells again, became agents of the devil. What the doctor said was good for us was never questioned. The tumors grew and we around them, licking at dust on grandmother's Bible and listening to the ache of errs our mouths had become.

Things I Liked About Gary

.....

To her second wedding my mother wore red. I wore red to my funeral, she'd say later.

The things I liked about Gary were this: he drew houses for me and let me borrow his pens, he drew houses and said he'd build my mother one, that *he'd* never live in a trailer. He had five kids from his first marriage; the youngest, Delia, was three years older than me. He had a station wagon the color of sky that was good without seatbelts for long car trips. He had a "house in the mountains" that he'd drive us to on weekends. In the car I'd leave the window rolled down and let the wind whip my hair into a mess I couldn't run my fingers through.

Gary told me a story about a boy sledding a hillside cornfield that had been mown. Dried stalks, broken at eight or ten inches tall, still marked the field where they'd been chopped. The boy hit a bump and went flying, landed with his face in a stalk. When he pulled himself up on his knees his eye pulled out of his head, attached to the stalk sticking out of the ground.

"The field is haunted," Gary told me, "that boy's eye still looks at you as you walk through the field." It was the same field where Gary's father died when his John Deere rolled over on him. I was afraid to ask why it wasn't haunted by him.

The night Gary's first wife left him his two adult sons held him by the arms. He'd threatened to cut his wife's head off and kick it down the hill into the creek behind their house. My mother and Gary met three weeks later in a bar.

The wedding was held eight months after that in the Methodist church, where we'd been to services exactly twice before. At the ceremony my brother sat stiffly in his pressed pants and clip-on tie, thinking about Dad. I sat with Delia in the front pew.

Gary's pants were a little too tight, and short as a result. My mother wore a red dress, her slip showing. She was eight months pregnant.

Delia and I laughed and laughed.

Bruising

.....

Some people burn their lover's letters when their heart gets broken. Or burn them years later when they've finally gotten over everything. I drown mine. Put them in the tub with me once the water has lost its heat, but before it grows too cold. As my fingers wilt and the bath bubbles level out into nothing but honey-scented film that greases the tub walls, I put my book or magazine down and pick up a letter I want to kill.

I unfold the sheets of paper. Double-sided are the best. I love watching the words from one side melt into words from the other, the paper fading to translucent, the water clouding bluely as it licks against the love.

When I was twelve or thirteen a boy named Jim almost drowned in our pool. Mother and Gary had people over and all of the adults were drunk or quickly getting there. Jim was four or five and couldn't swim, though he liked to hold up everybody's fun by standing on the diving board. He liked the bounce, the creaking. He liked boasting that if he really wanted to dive in he could. Said he'd be just fine.

After the third or fourth time he did this, my sister pushed him. The splash was almost silent, like he knew just how to get in. Like he'd done it all his short life, and gracefully. I almost believed that he could swim.

He sank to the bottom, fish-eyes wide, looking up, still. He lay there like he was already dead or still sleeping, like he hadn't woken up that day at all. The steady ripple of the water made his legs appear to undulate kelp-like from where we stood.

I dove in and pulled him out, amazed and breathless at how heavy a four-year-old boy could be. As soon as I touched him he came alive down there, scrambling in the sodden leaves on the pool's floor. By the time we surfaced he'd kicked me in the thigh and stomach and had reached up through my t-shirt to grab a fistful of my hair.

Jim never came over again. Whether this was by his choice or his parents' I never found out. But he always stared at our house when he rode by in the backseat of his parents' car and stared me down whenever he saw me, like I might steal his breath back if he looked away.

Perfect Score

.....

In the fourth grade it was Mike Kane. I thought of him as "Michael" because I'd heard his mother call him that once and it sounded softer. Miss Delniro put 100 percents on her "Star Board" and Michael's spelling tests were always there. Always there until the end of the school day they'd been posted. After everyone else had run for buses or started walking home, I would pull the thin strip of his perfect score out from under the gold thumbtack and slip it into the pocket of my jeans. When I got home I would run my fingers over the gray smudges the side of his left-handed hand had made as he rode across his words and marvel at the imperfections of his cursive. His "b's" and "d's" were always backwards, erased, and done again to complete the list to spelled perfection.

In the sixth grade it was Danny Owens. I'm not sure whether the jean jacket drew me in, or the constant reminder he gave that everyone call him "Maverick" after the Tom Cruise character in *Top Gun*, or the way he always smelled faintly like Cracker Jacks. I imagined him sweet and salty. Imagined my tongue moving from his mouth to neck and shoulders, to his fingers. I imagined him sticky and sweet, scenting my face and hands as they roved through his soft brown hair and down the back of that jean jacket he never took off. Near the end of the year we passed in the stairwell at school. He invited me to a Bon Jovi concert that weekend, said he had an extra ticket and would I like to go. I was so scared I said no immediately, nearly barked it. Before he even finished his sentence I had passed down half a flight of stairs.

Amy Everett couldn't spell and wore clothes that didn't fit her. I wanted to run my hands over her long brown hair. I inhaled deeply whenever she passed me in the hall. Of my crushes she's the first I'd ever been friends with. It felt different to have seen her in her underwear. Of my crushes she's the least I understood. I liked her because I had no power over my thoughts of her. I felt like I'd be locked away for the way I looked at her in gym class when she stretched the t-shirt out of her shorts. The pale white of her belly screamed at me under the gymnasium lights. But no one ever saw me look, too concerned as they were with their own clothes, weight, hair and nails. When girls were too busy looking at themselves I stared at them, opening them with my eyes the way I wanted to with my hands, to see what was inside.

Rule of Thirds

.....

Today my girlfriend and I had sex while a man took pictures in the backyard, I start, in a letter to my mother. This letter is not really intended for her, though when I start I pretend it is.

I do not say that the man was taking pictures of the deck he built and that we were having sex in the front room of the house, out of sight (though maybe not of earshot) of the man taking pictures in back. I do not mention that we met on my lunch break from work and that it felt like an illicit affair to meet in the middle of the afternoon. I do not mention the darkness of the front room, the front blue room with the dark starred fabric tacked over the window. I do not mention the sound of a man outside struggling with his dog who has decided right there in front of the house, the house we just moved into together, that he will not budge, that he cannot possibly take another step forward. "Doug," says the man, speaking briskly to the dog. "Doug." We laughed to hear the name and the man had no idea that a pretty girl was sitting squat over the face of another pretty girl just fifteen feet from where he and Doug were not moving.

I do not mention either in the letter the sound of birds, fighting or making love in the magnolia tree that bends low from the neighbor's yard into ours. I do not mention the brief flicker of red light against the starry fabric from an ambulance passing, that quiet brightness. I do not mention either that the man taking pictures out back came to the front door as we were kissing goodbye, kissing violently, arms pressed to bruising, fingers finding ribs and spinal notches and pressing as though those buttons did something useful. They are not useful in any way.

Whores

.....

When I was small I had a friend who hated her mother for adopting her.

"My real mother's a whore," she said.

"What's that?" I asked about the word "whore," though I didn't know what adoption meant either.

We sat Indian-style on a quilt on my bed that my grandmother had made for me when I was small. Bright-colored swatches with patterns of flowers met at complicated intersections where the lip of some pieces lifted off the quilt due to wear.

I ran my finger under a blue and white piece of fabric that had thinned. I liked to run the fabric under my fingernail and feel it there, to wet my fingers and curl them dry back and forth, back and forth over the baby blue, to see it tighten into a cigarette shape that I could pretend to smoke, dipping my head to the bed, smiling at Cathy. Each time I sucked the laundry smell into my lungs and held a moment, two moments, before letting go. I didn't tell Cathy I knew how to inhale. I made imaginary smoke rings like my mother's boyfriend did, but nobody saw them but me.

"What's a whore?" I asked her.

Cathy didn't answer. "I never met her. But I hear there's lots like me around, all from the same mother."

Suddenly I imagined the babies my mother must have been hiding, wondered if I would know them if they passed on the street. Would I know them in the checkout line? Would Mother admit to them if they called her *Mother*, would she take them home and raise them? I didn't know yet how babies worked. That they belonged to no one after the nine months in the womb.

Anything You Can Do

Natural Selection

.....

It was fantastic the way the sun showed all their flaws, the neighborhood women out in the light like something exposed. Standing around picnic tables like witches at cauldrons, dipping chips into batter that smelled like onions and eggs, drinking iced tea while men drank beer out of sweating cans, women in long fingernails, clickering along the edge of the bowl, feeling around for a napkin while they chattered with bits of chips and celery etched around their mouths. I didn't know their names, had never seen most of them. But I knew their men. I'd seen them looking. I walked Benny in the evening when the men took the kids to the playgrounds. I put Ben on my hip and set out walking as the sidewalk blued into night and the houses began to glow orange and yellow against the darkness.

Somehow that afternoon we ended up at the barbeque. A flier had gone around and Taft thought it might be nice to socialize. Benny was almost two and I had just learned I was pregnant with Carrie. Taft pushed Ben on the swing. I could hear his little cackle as he hit the high points, his ahs as he rolled through in forward motion. His blonde hair looked almost red in the sun, I remembered. I never saw that red again. I never looked.

Taft pushed him higher and they were completely absorbed, completely gone. A solid unit of two small cackling men.

"Can you watch Joanna just a moment?" some woman asked, thrusting her child into my arms. "I have to run home for something and she just gets into everything. The terrible twos turned into the dreadful threes."

She smiled and I tried to place her, if I knew her, where I knew her from. If we'd ever had a conversation before I could not recall it. And here I was, the sticky of her child, sweet washing over me. I thought of the woman in terms of husband as she walked away, tried to picture her with a man.

I stood halfway between the swing set where Taft and Benny and three or four other children played, stood halfway between them and the rest of the party. Women in cotton dresses laughing as they fingered food, men sweating into polyester shirts with collars splayed like wings. I leaned against a tree, feeling the child's weight pulling down on me, her fat legs cradling the new baby lodged inside me.

"You're heavier than you look," I said into the top of her curly dark hair. She smelled like lemons; her skin felt like a licked lollipop against my skin.

"Which one is your father?" I asked her.

"Pancake," the girl said, clapping her hands then pulling on her hair.

"Daddy," I said. "Dada. Which one is he, sweetheart?"

The girl made a sound like an engine starting and kicked her legs. I leaned forward, pushing my back against the tree to leverage myself. The girl kicked again and I dropped her. I heard Benny *ah*-ing in the air, Taft laughing loud out at the world the way he did when he was sure he owned it. I heard men sizzling steaks and drinking beer. I heard the women speaking, but could not make sense of anything they said. I heard a train somewhere far off moving out of town. Leaves blowing sounded like water on sand. Someone talked loudly, setting off a chorus of shouts in return. And the little girl fell.

I did not try to catch her. I didn't know I should. Her leg turned as she fell. Her curly black head hit twice on an exposed root.

She looked shocked for half a minute. Then she began to cry.

I imagined men and women rushing in to take her. To whisk the girl and Taft and Benny away. But no one noticed.

After a few good wails a couple of women looked our way. I set the girl on her feet, felt the back of her head at the lump growing there. I set her on her feet and she took off running, crying, weaving back and forth as she ran as though she too were trying to dodge a bullet. I did not see her mother. Another woman turned and stared, started toward the child.

"Taft," I called out to my husband, "let's go home." He reached a hand out, slowed the swing, bringing Ben back to earth, and I held Taft's hand as he led me there.

The Devastating Energy of Children

.....

With paper hats on their heads, Carrie and Delia danced to ABBA, their skirts hiked up a few inches and tucked into the waistbands of their panties to free their knees into movement.

Gary had had a lot to drink and danced with my sister who put her head on his shoulder as she looked at other guys. Delia threw flowers at their feet while Carrie twirled around them, staring into the air. She asked the DJ to play Cher and danced alone then because most people were over Cher by then or didn't know how to dance to "Dark Lady" without looking like fools.

I danced too, but mostly with other men. Gary's drinking buddies and people from work, a few of his cousins. When Carrie's pick cleared the dance floor I packed up my purse and headed to the ladies room to readjust my face and wait for a better song.

When I came back out Carrie was putting on a show, lifting her skirt as she turned circles. Red on the dance floor, hot under the lights, pale pink eight-year-old skin glowing like she'd never age.

Dark Lady laughed and danced and lit the candles one by one. Clap-clap.

And everyone watched her. All the men in the room. Gary. He smiled drunkenly like she was his. Delia on his lap clapping along.

I waited until the song ended. Of course. I didn't want to cause a scene. The song changed and Blondie came on. "Heart of Glass." Carrie started up twirling again. The floor filled with dancers. A man I'd never seen before took Carrie by both hands and swung her around. Put her down. Went back to dancing with his date. I approached her, my daughter, both of our hair rimmed with red light flashing to blue.

"Come with me."

"What?" She continued dancing as though she hadn't heard. I yanked her arm gently at first, pulled her off the floor.

"Sit down over there." I pointed to the food table where everyone was done. Punch sloshed red like muted blood stains across the top of it.

"Why?" she whined like she had a right to. "I want to dance."

"It's for grownups now." I turned and Gary looked at us, started to get up, sat back down.

"But—"

"You heard me. Behave."

She looked back at the other kids under the lights, coupled up or dancing with parents, swinging their weak little arms with the devastating energy of children.

"Go," I told her. I wanted to hit her, but didn't. I just wanted her to sit her ass down. To not ruin my good time with her foreplay.

It's not that I felt I had a right to control her, it's like she wanted me to.

I gave Gary a blowjob in the men's room before returning to the dance floor.

Delia shuttled glasses of Merlot into the corner with Carrie and they pretended the sides of their fists were boys' mouths. Then they made believe the other girl was a boy and practiced kissing that way, practiced wedding kisses, their mouths raw with wine.

"You may now kiss the bride."

"You may now kiss the bride."

And they did, over and over again.

Wedding Fingers

.....

What is it about girls that they just naturally slip found rings over their tiny wedding fingers? If you left a ring on the floor of an empty room, its small glint casting a tiny shadow on the floor and sent a little boy in, he would spin it or stick it in his teeth, see if he could bite it down into something, make it into something. A girl would put it on her finger, slip it down gently, loosely over bony joints of those fleshy little fingers. She would imagine, too, the man who would give it to her. I imagined my father's friends first, before anything, the way they smelled, the way they smiled. Then men on TV who already had wives with frilly dresses and perfect hair. I imagined men who towered over me.

Why did I have to see her there? Fooling with things on top of Terry's dresser? On tip-toes in the bedroom he and I shared. On tip-toes, flat chest against the dark wood of the dresser, against the patinaed knobs. Barefoot and standing on his thick boots. Barefoot standing on her tip-toes. Her white legs with a question mark of dirt on the back of one knee. Or maybe a bruise. She fingered the change there, pressed pennies and dimes down with her fingers, slid them around. She touched the belt buckle like it burned, the snake of leather coiled around it, looped and pressing in. The night before, he'd tied my arms with it. In a second I was back to that, then saw her there again and wondered what she thought of as she touched it. What the burn was, the pulling away? Was it the hot memory of a hand over her mouth?

And then she found it. Just some small ring he had no use for. One he wore on his pinky once in a while. A solid band with a jagged design that meant nothing, *was* nothing. She reached for it, sliding things aside, pushing the belt, buckle scratched against the wood like a closet door sliding open. She reached for it, fumbled, tipped it up on its side so it came rolling at her, fast. She caught it in one hand as it tumbled off the side, caught it in one hand and rolled back on her heels. She laughed a little to have caught it like that. Laughed to say, *I got it*. I could almost hear her. Hear the words inside her. She looked at it, turned it around in the midday yellow of the room like some young appraiser with glass wedged in her eye, squinted. Then she slipped it on her finger, ring finger, left hand. Slipped it down and looked at it. Fanned her hand out in front of her. More delicate than I'd ever seen her be. More girl. In that moment, too like me.

The front door slammed open, Terry home. Carrie and I both started. I backed up in the hall, out of Carrie's sight. And she came running from the room. Yelling "Daddy!" like she never did. Like she looked sheepish, did right by us when she'd done something wrong. Terry, 19 or 20 then to my 32, wanted them to call him Daddy and they never did. She yelled *Daddy* and fell into his arms.

The Terminal

.....

We walked the terminal silently and I found myself wanting to touch her hair or shoulder with the palm of my hand. My small, tanned, untouchable child.

The intercom crackled intermittently over us, but it wasn't enough. I smoked cigarette after cigarette to keep my hands busy. While on the train between terminals, where smoking had just become prohibited, I twisted my hair around two fingers of one hand and drummed the other against my purse.

Against the side of the train, doubled in the glass's reflection stood a mother with her daughter in front of her, the mother's arms crisscrossed against the girl's shoulder blades. They looked alike a little bit, and the father stood next to them, holding the metal bar above his head, his shoulders and back encumbered by the family luggage. He was vaguely handsome and I tried to catch his eye, if only to comment silently on his apparent success as a family man. He talked in quiet tones, the mother smiled, the daughter I think met Carrie's eyes. They were about the same age, eleven years old. But maybe she was twelve then.

The train stopped. I asked, "Baggage claim?" The girl stepped out of her mother's embrace.

Carrie patted her duffle bag. "This is it," she said.

"I forget you pack light."

"Yes," she said. I could hear in her the distraction of having expected these extra minutes to herself and the frustration of not having them, of having to speak too soon. Could see her hanging on to the last vestiges of what she would probably call freedom, staring at the flicker of a fluorescent light, watching the canter of a small child trailing after its grandparents, a man pausing to pick up a piece of paper dropped by a young woman, unfold and read its contents before hurrying up behind her to hand it back.

I was sorry I had come to the gate.

She'd been lost once in an airport when she was six, traveling alone. Lost in O'Hare. The airline called and said they'd lost her. They were blunt about it. Only they made the statement in a way that removed all responsibility, instead of saying we lost her, they only said she's lost.

We passed through the glass doors and out into the parking garage. The humidity swept over us.

"I got my period," she said.

"Really?" I asked. "How'd your father take that?" I laughed because she had smiled suddenly and it seemed okay.

"He didn't. He called every woman in town he'd ever known until he got one willing to come over to discuss my 'options.' By then I had already walked to the store and bought tampons."

What she didn't tell me is that she spent two weeks in Mexico, in a small town on the eastern coast of Baja, with a few kids she'd met in San Francisco, on the boat to Alcatraz, a group of teenaged boys and two or three girls, who ditched their summer jobs to ride to the island prison that day because in all their years in San Francisco they'd never been there, who ditched their summer jobs the next two weeks after hatching a plan in some damp cell that they should pool their money and borrow someone's sister's Subaru. That they piled it full of beef jerky and bottled water, boxes of sugared cereal and bags of chips and set off for the border three days later. She didn't tell me she went with them, that she didn't tell her father. That they stayed in a cabana motel one block from the beach, in a town of 300, none of whom spoke English, and none of them spoke Spanish, only enough to say *hola, amigo, cerveza, inglés*. That they stayed for thirty dollars per week, which worked out to less than a dollar per kid per day. That the water ran out on the fourth day and so they substituted cheap Mexican beer and tequila to keep their mouths wet. They had heard nothing of Mexico but that you shouldn't drink the water, so they didn't. That they swam every afternoon, spreading sunscreen over burning bodies, and naked every night, lighting bonfires beachside to swim by. That one girl got dragged home two days into the trip when her mother found out where she was. She didn't tell me that she slept with three of the five boys and two in just one night. That she let them fuck her because she liked the way they smelled after swimming, when the salt water replaced their boy smells and made them taste like men.

Waiting, Watching the Ocean

.....

Somewhere on the West Coast, beach front, overlooking the ocean and some fist-sized stones that pass for beach, Carrie sits in her car, windows rolled up, feeling the heat of a summer afternoon, sweating into her tank top, sweating into her underwear. She's in the beach park overlook sweating inside her car. Yellow jackets hover around the side mirrors, smack into the window from time to time, beating themselves in the heat repeatedly, then buzzing circularly and drifting away. It's as though the wind catches them. Or they remember—suddenly—something they must get back to. Carrie sits inside her car, sweat beading her temples and itching as the beads travel down her cheeks and her neck.

Waiting. She doesn't even think this to herself. She doesn't even know. She's waiting. With the windows rolled up she thinks of greenhouses. She thinks of Southern summers and how the heat could kill her there, had tried to kill her. She went four summers in Georgia with no a/c in her car. When she got off work at five the hot box of her Volvo threatened to spoil her, to melt her skin like wax against flame.

She's waiting, watching the ocean. Watching the gulls fly and dive. Watching the faint outline of a kite ducking and twirling on a taut string.

Buzz, and another tap on the window. She sees her face outlined in the glass. A man pulls up in a pickup truck alongside. No children. No dogs or anything. He's young, late thirties. She sizes him up without looking directly at him. Neat, even hair, stubbled chin and cheeks. A man who could grow a full beard. He's summer-dark, suntanned, with hair like little black knives on his arms.

Fourteen spaces on the unpaved lot, white car and white pickup side by side. A kite down the beach. The lapping of waves play, soft white noise, static. A dog barks a ways down the beach. All of this muted through the glass.

Carrie leans back. What a woman's made for. Reaches into her jeans. The man looks. The man looks away. Looks.

She thinks. This is what he came here for. This is what he came to see. There's a reason he's not gotten out of his car. She leans back, turns her head slightly into the shot of sun, threatens to look at him, doesn't.

Carrie pauses, adjusts. Undoes the top button of her jeans, unzips halfway down. Slow, like she means it. Pushes into the underside of the steering wheel, thrusting out like she's thrusting. Pushes down her jeans. Eases the thick of the jeans over her ass and sits back down.

She stares at the water, counts four, five, six sails on the shock of white, sun-stabbed horizon, seven. She cannot see the waves, but never forgets they're there, keeping time with the bees jittering intermittently against the window. She cannot see the waves or the stones on the beach, fists knocking together. Cannot see the sharp crags where the people sit in the sun.

Sun through the windshield paints her skin stark white with a blue strip across her neck and chin from tinted upper edge of glass.

She smiles. She has no idea why she's never thought of this before.

She stays just like this, jeans down just to the crotch of her panties, the ones she knows show her pubic hair through.

She looks at the man for the first time, long enough to see his eyes, then looks away. *Blue*, her look says, *are you with me?*

She thumbs the window down just a crack, enough to slip a hand through. Four fingers and a thumb. Just enough to breathe. Shirt wet, she runs her hand inside, pauses at the nipple where she should. Looks at the man and slips her hand inside her underwear.

A yellow jacket smacks the window four times before stumbling inside. It moans and mumbles inside the glass.

Getting Help

.....

After all of it, I act like someone conquered—shuffling photographs on the mantle, putting dishes away—rather than what I am, someone who moves. Exterior is all performance. The weight of what's inside could swallow this house and town and entire planet whole, but it doesn't exist. *Es besteht nicht. Ich bestehe nicht.* What doesn't exist could kill a lesser woman.

My sister suggested I go see someone after Glenn died. And so I did.

Psychotherapy hooked me. Intoxicated with that focused set of eyes on me in a room, I liked the heat of the desk lamp, liked the sterile walls, the sunshine dependent on the will of open shades. The small man with hands that looked just strong enough to hold around a woman's neck. Not enough to chop wood. Just to hold her down.

The first was Dr. Macgregor, Irish, petite, reddish hair, nothing on his face but features. Nothing holding his body up but the slant of the chair and the starch in his clothes. He was nothing, a silence. I sat silent, too. We played with the silent smell in the room, newly washed windows and cellophane, unopened books, aftershave and lemon, coffee, cellophane.

The second one was Dr. Stevens. Tall and brutish. He smiled, which told me he was no good for me. A smiling man will never win my trust. But I returned for the heat of attention. I thought, no relationships for me, I will sit in this room and have a man listen. I will think about his hands on me, bruising my arms, my throat. I will think about the way he fucks. I will think of his thick, smiling face fucking down into another body. I will sit back and we will smile together.

The whole time I sat before Dr. Stevens I was a body, naked, propped up in a chair.

"What do you want to talk about today, Victoria?"

"The way you say my name."

He said nothing.

I wondered as I said something—

"I resent my job."

"What do you mean?"

"I resent *having* a job."

—how I looked to him saying it. How he thought he looked speaking back. If he wondered about that. If he rubbed his forefinger and middle finger over his watch face just to see me squirm.

I crossed my legs. I uncrossed my legs. If he noticed, he didn't let on. I tried opening my legs a little, my skirt allowing in the cool air from the open window, the cool clinical air of the breeze washing over the bookshelves, wending over the implements on the desk that proved he did serious work there. Nothing.

"Have you ever thought about taking medication?" They all asked me this.

"No."

"You answered quickly, why?"

"I don't feel anything. I move around in a fog."

He let me get away with this, though I never specified if the fog was a side effect or the natural state I wasn't looking to change.

I feel nothing, I said. I was a wash of contradictions. What I meant to say is, I feel nothing and I am afraid of feeling nothing and my fear makes me angry.

Dr. Stevens didn't let me fall for him. The first one, the Irishman let me blow him while he stood on his rolling desk chair. Stevens referred me to someone else because I touched his cock through his khakis once when he showed me out.

"How am I to learn from any of this?"

"Dr. Kincaid is very good."

Dr. Kincaid's waiting room smelled like a goatherd. There were four chairs. I sat in the one farthest from the receptionist. I slipped a piece of chocolate from my purse and bit it slowly not for the taste, but to smell chocolate instead of goat. I flipped through *People* magazine. The wedding issue. Young girls in white dresses with million-dollar hair standing with old men or young men in million-dollar tuxedos. One man wore sandals, had ribbons in his hair. Two couples had babies already. On the back pages were records of recent divorce.

"Victoria?" A woman spoke. I always finish the sentence before looking up. "I can see you now."

I read on, turned the page.

"Victoria?"

The receptionist, who had taken my information, had clicked it all into her computer, stared up from her book. I felt them both. Four eyes rolled back into nothing. A pause on the clock.

"Am I running late?" Dr. Kincaid asked the girl behind the desk, searching for explanation to exonerate the woman holding the magazine. A magazine held in a waiting room stands as proof of waiting. We all knew this. I wondered if Dr. Stevens was gay.

"Victoria Jenkins?"

I looked at my watch. Or rather, wearing no watch, looked briefly at the wrist bone pushing up at my skin like a pillow under a blanket. One more look at the groom, the flowers in her hair, the wave curling on forever behind the happy couple getting married on the beach.

I stood and left the room.

"Thank you." The girl behind the desk spoke out of automation. The door hissed shut behind me. The sound of a woman speaking under her breath.

Shoulder

.....

I land on my feet; it's what I do. I convince my youngest, Evie, to drive north with me, through Georgia to South Carolina. We drive through Barnwell, through Bamberg County. We travel back roads only because that's all there is. In small towns we count stop signs, count roads, intersections, look for the post office to tell us the name. It's always on the way, on the same road we're on, the main road through town.

Tufts of cotton tremble by the roadside. Truck-sized bales cast shadows across the fields. Dust blows like snow and I dream of winter. Dust blows and I dream of tornados topping the car and lifting off. We stop at diners and lardy kitchens where they serve meat and three, every side dish leaves pools of grease on chipped plates. Evie dabs at her string beans with paper napkins folded and picks out bits of pork.

"I don't know what we're doing here," she says. "I don't know why I came."

"To spend time with your mother."

Neither one of us mentions her compensation, that I'm paying her to be here, to ride shotgun on this road trip through the dirt backside of the South, this place where we came from.

"You know you have relatives here, Eve?"

"Nobody I know."

"Fact is probably all these people are related to us."

"Are you going to start talking about how we're all God's children?"

I laugh as we drive past another field of something turning green to brown in the late summer heat. Four dark men stand at a piece of rusted machinery, smoking cigarettes and digging into the engine with their hands. Two children ride by on a bicycle, the bigger boy lifts out of the seat, pumping hard. His shirt flies out behind him, cape-like in the wind.

"What about them?" Evie says.

"Who?"

"Any of them."

"Probably."

"What do you know about any of this?"

We get to the next town and the next town. Wisteria covers everything, vines like cancer over everything, houses, trees, fences, climbing up clotheslines, telephone poles. Three parked cars in three yards in a row even had vines growing over.

"Why do they do that here?" Evie asks.

"What?"

"Leave cars on the lawn."

"They do that everywhere."

"Not in Jacksonville."

"Everywhere. People use them for parts, they work on their own cars. People have trouble letting things go."

"Whatever."

"Kids play in them."

"I've never played in a car parked on somebody's lawn."

"You've never done a lot of things."

"Oh, I've done a lot of things. Probably more than you know."

"So have I," I say to her.

"What have you done?"

"Mostly everything."

"That's a lie," Evie says, laughing.

I don't know what to say. I want to push her out of the car. I imagine her on the roadside. I imagine her thumbing a ride, peering into cars, waiting for the right one, the white one. I imagine her scared like she's never been scared before.

"Surprise me," she says.

"I had an abortion."

She says nothing. She stares out the window. I look at her, she's shrugging her shoulders slightly. Maybe crying, maybe not.

"Evie?"

"Fuck you."

"What?"

"Fuck you," she says. "Fuck you, I want to go home."

"Fuck you, too," I say.

"I don't have to tell you everything."

"What are you talking about?"

"Is that what this is about?"

"Evie, what are you talking about?"

"I don't have to tell you everything," she says. "You should really get your own friends."

Wisteria blooming with visible tumors, white and purple, everywhere. Everywhere. The signs are painted perfectly by the side of the road. The houses are painted perfectly. Impeccable signs by the side of the road. Signs for everything. Specials painted into the windows. Specials on meat, on carrots, on greens, green beans, paper towels. The next window, the next window, specials on baby clothes, evening clothes, pianos, rabbits. You can get everything everywhere in America. You can find it all here. The lines on the road line up perfectly, perpendicular to the car. Welcome to America. The white and the yellow, pushing in.

A woman on the sidewalk walks behind a stroller, two children face front, staring through the heat, red from the weather. The woman's hair is in curls; as we slow for the stop sign I hear the ticking of her sandals on the pavement. Evie has cracked her window.

"God, I'm dying in here."

So am I, I want to tell her. So am I.

The woman turns to cross. I start to let the foot off the brake. Then I don't. I let her go.

"What an ugly shirt," I say as she crosses. "What was she thinking to go out of the house dressed like that?"

"She looks like a disaster." Evie rolls up the window, smiles, jacks up the a/c.

I say nothing and roll through the next three stops. The heat sleeps, shimmer on the pavement, shimmer on the hood of the car.

About the Author

.....

Elizabeth J. Colen is the author of prose poetry collection *Money for Sunsets* (Steel Toe Books, 2010). She resides in the Pacific Northwest, is poetry editor of *Thumbnail Magazine*, and occasionally blogs at www.elizabethjcolen.blogspot.com.

Evan's House and the Other Boys Who Live There

:::: *Tim Jones-Yelvington* ::::

ACKNOWLEDGMENTS

"To Be a Friend Is to Make a Friend" as "Friends" *Titular*

"Wherein the Purple Thermos Confronts the Edge" as "Untitled" *Six Sentences*

"Slime Me" *Necessary Fiction*

"Painted Faces" *Keyhole* and *Skip, Patch, Eye, Brownie, Chalk: Coming of Age Stories* (Bannock Street Books)

"Brendan Kills" *decomP*

"American Kids" *Mud Luscious*

"Grace" *The Legendary*

"Unnecessary" *Everyday Genius*

"Fugitives" *Pank*

"What if the Dungeon Closes" *Smokelong Quarterly*

Table of Contents

Evan's House and the Other Boys Who Live There

Cast of Boys (In Order of Appearance)

Boy Who Is Not a Boy, but Evan's House
Boy Who Makes His Friends
Boy Who Is Timmy, and Covets the Purple Thermos
Boy Who Is Abner, and Wants to Get Slimed
Boy Who Is Evan, and Loves His Mom
Boy Who Wants to Paint His Face
Boy Who Is Evan, and Plays the Recorder
Boy Who Loves Brendan
Boy Who Is Bristol, and Sometimes Levi
Boy Who Is Evan, and Loves Stephen
Boy Who Loves Kevin
Boy Who Is Evan, Crashing with Kandace
Boy Who Steals Soda
Boy Who Is Not a Boy, but Evan's Mother
Boy Who Has a Batty Mother
Boy Who Is Patrick, Evan's Boyfriend
Boy Who Flips His Shit
Boy Who Thinks He Isn't the Fugitive
Boy Who Is Not a Boy, but Evan's House (reprise)
Boy Who Hangs with a Dominatrix

House

Boy Who Is Not a Boy, but Evan's House

.....

This is a picture of Evan's house, a picture of me. I am Evan's house. Evan drew his mother this picture in school today, the first day of third grade. Look closely. There are details you won't want to miss. Notice, for instance, the color of my roof, an unusual combination of deep purple and green Evan made by alternating and then blending his crayons. The green, Evan tells his mother, is mold. Mold makes his mother sneeze.

Evan's father has never lived inside me. He lived in Evan's last house, when he was married to Evan's mother. Now Evan visits him at one of those two-story 1960s apartment complexes that resemble a Motel 6. Evan sleeps on his couch. The dust makes Evan sneeze.

Look at my driveway. There are no cars. Evan tells his mother it's because she went to a meeting. (Her work in the nonprofit sector places regrettable demands on her time.)

"What about the babysitter's car?" his mother asks.

"The babysitter doesn't drive," Evan says. "She lives nearby."

Evan's father left Evan's last house, the one he shared with Evan's mother, when Evan was three years old. The last day he lived there, he slapped Evan's mother across the cheek, only once, and only to get her to stop yelling. Evan used to remember this. He used to pound his fist into his hand and repeat, "Daddy hit Mommy."

Look at my front yard. A series of multicolored blobs cluster around a bright yellow rectangle. Those blobs are stuffed animals, Evan says. Evan's mother asks about the yellow rectangle, and about the white boxes beside each animal.

"That yellow thing's a table," Evan says. "Those white things are agendas. The animals are having a meeting."

Whenever Evan comes to visit, the first thing his father does is throw his clothes into the trash. He throws away the clothes Evan's mother has purchased and replaces them with clothes he chose, knowing this will upset her.

Look at my front door. Look at Evan as a stick figure, standing on the stoop.

Evan's mother pulls out a manila folder to stow Evan's drawing neatly in her briefcase. She plans to mount the drawing on her office bulletin board, so everybody will see how her son considers her needs. From his stoop, stick figure Evan is waving as she carries him away. Wave back. Wave to stick figure Evan. Wave.

To Be a Friend Is to Make a Friend

Boy Who Makes His Friends

.....

No one spoke to me. I hid behind my desk coloring neon hairdos on rock stars. When I asked my mother how to make friends, she pulled a framed needlepoint from a bureau: *To be a friend is to make a friend.* She said, "Never forget that."

I met a boy named Billy, sitting on the snow mounds at the edge of the elementary school parking lot. I parroted my mother's needlepoint and he said, "That's not how you make a friend. To make a friend, you say Hi, my name is Billy. I like to play with Ninja Turtles and slide down the stairway in my snow pants. What do you like to do?"

Billy and I christened the snow mounds the secret nation of Snowvakia. We held a coronation ceremony and named Billy Snowvakia's sovereign. I colored a picture of King Billy and I on the mound, fighting off the dreaded fanged mountain goats of Snowvakia with sabers carved from ice.

The next year, when I said hello to Billy in the hallway, he looked the other way.

.....

My best friend Scott and I became superheroes. I was Turquoise Man. I wore turquoise sweats, turquoise Converse, turquoise underwear and turquoise socks.

Scott played my loyal sidekick Fireball, but he didn't have a special costume. I imagined he wore bright red spandex. We battled our sworn enemy, the "Big Fat Lunch Lady." The Big Fat Lunch Lady yelled at the kids on the playground, "Be quiet!" I hated her for treating me like an ordinary child.

One day Scott showed up wearing his own turquoise sweat suit and said he wanted a turn as Turquoise Man. I didn't want to tell him his shirt and pants didn't match, so I said, "You should be Fireball. Fireball's cooler. Fireball shoots balls of fire from his hands."

Scott took me to his church one Sunday. Scott was Assembly of God. The pastor asked me to write my phone number on a piece of paper and called me the following Friday to invite me back. "We're Unitarian!" my mother said and slammed the receiver.

Scott moved to Phoenix and never sent a postcard.

Mike ran for student body president. I was Mike's campaign manager. I made a sign on the computer. I filled the background with vines and leaves and wrote a message: *Go for the jungular. Go for Mike!*

Mike was rail-thin and anxious. His head resembled a soccer ball balanced on a yardstick. His eyes roved the room like a gazelle's on a nature program, watching for lions. When he lost the election, he blamed it on our classmate Alexander.

One day I found fake blood in the costume cabinet in the high school auditorium. I thought it would be fun to play a prank, so I spilled the blood all over Mike's backpack and left a note: *I'm with you. I'm watching you. 666.*

Mike freaked so I told him I didn't know who did it. I helped him hack Alexander's email account. I helped him crack Alexander's locker combination. We followed Alexander through the hallway hoping to catch him in an incriminating act.

Our principal called me into his office. He said, "Did Mike pressure you to help frame Alexander?" He placed his palm on my lower back and rubbed it from side to side. He said, "You remind me of myself as a kid, small and awkward. We'd understand if you're helping Mike. You just have to tell us so we can catch him."

Mike was expelled.

Wherein the Purple Thermos Confronts the Edge

Boy Who Is Timmy, and Covets the Purple Thermos

.....

Britney the master skipper raps her stone against the rock and says, "Whoever skips a dozen stones fastest gets the purple thermos." Timmy fingers his zipper, knowing he is doomed and thinking purple would've looked so pretty with his yellow lunch pail. Britney's yellow pigtails bob in time with the buoys as she turns her back and traces a line in the sand. "Whoever crosses this line is out of bounds." Timmy throws the purple thermos on the ground and crushes it with his boot. Later, the tide takes the purple thermos to meet the edge of the sky.

Slime Me

Boy Who Is Abner, and Wants to Get Slimed

.....

Abner was a child who wanted to get slimed. He hungered for the spread of slime across his skin, his favorite the viscous kind that crept to cover, coat, encase. He oozed homemade do-it-yourself Mad Scientist slime though his fingers and hoped someone would cover him in goop.

He invited his best friend Elmer to play. A bit of booger always glistened beneath Elmer's nose, beckoned to Abner. How Abner longed for such an affliction! He watched Elmer lift his elbow and smother his booger with shirt. No! No! No! he thought, the waste! Wipe it on *me.* Drip it on *me.* Press your finger against your nostril and blow, blow hard in my direction.

He handed Elmer a cup of slime, lay on the floor and pulled up his shirt, exposed his taut tummy.

"Slime me," he said.

"Huh?"

"Slime me."

"I don't know how."

Abner looked up, hopeful, remembered the television show he watched where every time the actors said "I don't know," slime fell from the sky and slimed them.

He perched on his elbows, showed Elmer how to tip the cup.

"Now you try."

"I don't know..."

Abner thought about a different television show, where crime-fighting cartoon turtles got captured and chained to platforms beneath slowly descending slime. It was his favorite episode. He'd later wrapped shoelaces around his action figures and coated their heads and bodies in gooey green. He'd often scanned the channels in search of a rerun.

He pulled a bandana from his pocket and handed it to Elmer.

"Tie my hands," he said. "That way I can't escape."

"Maybe I should ask my mom first," Elmer said. "What if it's a sin?"

Elmer's parents were evangelicals. He'd brought Abner to numerous vacation Bible schools where clergy plied children with relay races then called them to the altar to accept Jesus into their hearts.

"It's not a sin," Abner said. "Even Jesus liked slime. I read it in Corinthians."

Elmer scrunched his nose. A fresh booger inched forward, and Abner's pulse quickened.

"No he didn't. You're lying."

"Please," Abner said. "Slime me."

"I can't," Elmer said. "I'm sorry, I can't."

"Please."

Elmer whipped his head around.

"I think I heard a horn honk," Elmer said, though Abner hadn't heard a thing. "I think it's my mom."

Elmer shuttled out the door, slammed it behind him. Abner got up, ran to the door and pressed his hands against the glass. He saw Elmer at the end of the block, disappearing behind a bush.

Abner pushed through the door.

"Wait!" Abner called. "Elmer!"

He chased Elmer around the block and down another, around a corner, through an alley, calling, "Elmer!"

Finally, he lost him at a four-way intersection.

Abner hunched, slapped his hands against his thighs, tried to breathe. He had an idea.

Abner ran, as quick as he could run, to Elmer's house, a good fifteen minutes from the intersection, even running. He stopped several times, out of breath, walked a block or two, continued to run. He sat down on Elmer's porch, certain he must have arrived before Elmer.

He waited. His chest still pounded. Where was Elmer? He waited some more. He tried to focus on the slime, how it would feel when Elmer at last poured it over him, how it would creep across his skin. He waited, still no Elmer. He stood up and walked around the side of the house. Elmer's bedroom window was too high to see into. Abner grabbed a chair from the backyard patio and climbed up. Elmer's blinds were drawn, but Abner thought he saw a flicker of motion through a crack.

"Elmer!" he shouted. "Elmer!"

"Abner?"

Elmer's mother stood where the house curved toward the front porch. She was wearing an apron.

"Abner, what are you doing here?"

Abner climbed off the chair.

"I'm- I- I was waiting for Elmer," he said. He looked at his feet and wanted to run in the other direction. "He left something at my house."

"Elmer came home twenty minutes ago," Elmer's mother said. Her voice was cheerful, but edged with suspicion. Abner remembered the stories Elmer told about getting punished, cleaning out the gutters. "Would you like me to go inside and get him?"

Abner nodded. He followed Elmer's mother to the front porch, where he waited while she went inside.

"I'm sorry," Elmer's mother said, when she returned. "Elmer says he isn't feeling well. Why don't you give me whatever he left behind."

Abner felt inside his pockets, but all he felt was his cup of slime. His cheeks grew hot. Facing Elmer's mother, he felt suddenly shamed by the only thing he wanted to do.

"I guess I forgot it," he mumbled.

"I'm sorry?"

"I forgot it," he said again, a bit louder.

"If you do not speak up, child, the Lord won't hear you."

"I- FOR- GOT- IT!"

"Now Abner," said Elmer's mother, sternly. "You needn't raise your voice."

Abner turned and ran as far as he could run and then kept running until he collapsed panting in somebody's yard, his back against a boulder. He wheezed. He thought he might cry. He fingered the cup of slime inside his pocket, removed it. He pulled up his shirt and held the cup above his navel. He tipped the cup. He watched the slime glob on its edge, then slowly drip. He felt it touch, a little sticky. But it wasn't enough, would never be enough, if he knew when the slime was coming and where it would fall. "Elmer," Abner said. He looked at the sky. "Slime me," he said to the sky, then, "I don't know," because he didn't, he really didn't know.

House of Mirth

Boy Who Is Evan, and Loves His Mom

.....

Evan's favorite childhood memory is of the time his mother's friend Frank came over and brought his fog machine. Frank plugged the fog machine into the wall and piped dry ice into the living room. Evan's mother hunched forward and dragged her fists against the floor. Then she arched her back, beat against her upper chest, and bellowed.

"I'm a gorilla," she said. "I'm a gorilla in the mist."

Evan giggled. His mother yodeled a tune from a musical they'd rented for one of their Friday night movie nights, when they spread a bath towel across the floor in front of the television and crunched potato chips dipped in plain sour cream.

"Brigadoon," she sang. "Brigadoon..."

Evan thinks about the fog machine after his mother hurls an X-Acto knife into the wall. She was cutting a strip of foam-core for Evan's class project, a diorama of an Anasazi cliff dwelling, when she lost her grip and sliced the foam-core into two useless halves. As it flies across the room, the X-Acto knife strikes a canister of sand Evan's mother purchased to affix to the cliff face. The sand spills across the living room floor. Evan's mother rises from the floor and pounds away. He hears her bedroom door slam.

It used to be, whenever Evan's mother lost her temper, she'd apologize. She'd say, "Someday you're going to tell your therapist about this, all about your crazy mother." And Evan would say, "No I'm not, you're perfect." And he would feel wonderful and useful for having reassured her.

Now that Evan's older, his mother never apologizes.

Painted Faces

Boy Who Wants to Paint His Face

.....

"If somebody gave you a hundred dollars, how would you use it?" Randy says. We're at the Clareborne County Mall. We're celebrating Randy's twelfth birthday. "Want to know how I'd use it?" he says. "Hookers!" We're standing near the face-painting kiosk. I want to dig my fingers into the paint and spread yellow whiskers across my cheeks. I want to become a lion. That's how I'd use the money. I don't want to tell Randy I still like painting my face. I don't want Randy to call me a baby. Or faggot. "Me too," I say. "Definitely hookers."

Schoolhouse Rock

Boy Who Is Evan, and Plays the Recorder

.....

I spent all week practicing, but I didn't get a perfect ten. I stood in front of the mirror in my bedroom and I held my recorder and played "When Johnny Comes Marching Home" over and over, until my fingers did just what they were supposed to do and I didn't play one note wrong. Then I went to school and tried to play it in front of everybody in my music class. I guess I knew seventh grade was too old to care about the recorder and still be cool, but it's nice to be good at something and I can't shoot a basket, because the ball goes all wonky and flies the other way. I stood in front of the class and started to play the song. Matt Balfurd was sitting behind me and I could hear him whisper. "Faggot," he said. My fingers landed in the wrong spot and the notes came out all wrong. I took the recorder and threw it against the ground, hard. The pieces came apart and rolled in different directions. "Bet I got something else you can blow," Matt Balfurd said. I picked up my back-pack and threw it right at Matt Balfurd's head. The other kids started making noises, like saying "ohhhhh" in that way where it starts out all low and ends up all high, like when someone's about to get in trouble or someone else wants to start a fight. "Evan!" the music teacher said. I couldn't look her in the face, so I ran out of the room. There's a spot at the very top of the stairway where nobody ever goes. It's by the door to the roof. I'm sitting here while I wait. I can hear them calling my name, but I won't come down until they find me. I'll make them look for me. And then they'll have to ask what's wrong.

Brendan Kills

Boy Who Loves Brendan

.....

Brendan murders the nigger bitch. That's what he calls it when he beats Serena at tennis, on his Wii. "Die, bitch," he says, and swipes his controller.

"What?" he says. "We can say that shit now, we got a black president."

I know it should bother me, him using that word. I watch him pant and curse and jab the remote, the violence of him, the stink. Brendan beats his Wii. It tents my pants. I'm not a nigger bitch, I'm just another teenage white boy like Brendan, but sometimes Brendan calls me one, and these are my favorite times. "Burn, bitch," Brendan says, and drives his cigarette's lit tip into my lower back until I buck and thrash. Brendan keeps his hair in a box. It isn't a special hand-carved heirloom or anything, it's just a beat-up cardboard box, like the kind they use to ship envelopes. The hair is from last year, when we were freshmen, when Brendan cut off his ponytail. He keeps it coiled, braided and banded. He bends me onto my knees, and he binds my hands behind my back, and then he stuffs the braid inside my mouth while he grinds the cigarettes into my ass, my thighs, my shoulders. Then I suck him off until he shoots and I swallow.

Brendan hates how much he likes it when I suck him. He says he only does it because we're in high school, and high school girls are prudes, but I can tell he wants it, it wouldn't be the same with a girl. This is Brendan's shame, the boy thing. My shame is everything else. I think sometimes I should stop, but then I hear Brendan curse and I smell him, and I get so hard I think I'll explode into pieces tiny enough to fit in Brendan's box. And when I think about this, Brendan carrying me around forever and ever, in pieces, pressed up against his braid, I feel tingly and warm.

American Kids

Boy Who Is Bristol, and Sometimes Levi

.....

Bristol likes Levi to fuck her with his hockey mask on, behind a tree in the church courtyard. She likes to pretend he's a rapist. Levi takes advantage, and Bristol takes Levi, takes the Lord's name in vain, takes hold of a tree branch cracked by the force of her grip, screaming, "Oh my fucking Christ. Stopitstopit stop."

Levi likes when Bristol stands outside the Yukon Creamery, sucking hot dogs with relish. He likes to pretend he's a hockey star and Bristol is his groupie. In the parking lot outside the stadium, she begs him for it. He likes the way her name sounds thrust through his mouth.

"Bristo-oh-oh-oh-ohhhhh---"

There's a game all the kids play at the church on Sundays, to pass the time in the pews. Take the name of a hymn, any hymn, and add the words "between the sheets."

Christ the Lord Has Risen Today ...between the sheets.

How Great Thou Art ...between the sheets.

O Thou Sacred Head Now Wounded ...between the sheets.

Whenever Bristol hears the word "Bible," she pictures belts. She knows the Bible Belt is somewhere in the lower 48, but she imagines it stretches across the North Slope, a belt of sacred oil. She pictures a belt with an enormous gold buckle. This is the belt she pictures her mother holding when she realizes she's late. Twenty lashes from the Bible Belt and she'll be saved.

"Fucking Christ!" Levi says when she tells him. "Fucking babies? Are you fucking with me?"

"God bless America," the Mother stumps. "God bless our children."

She perches, imperious. Watchers wonder whether the distinction between the podium and the pulpit is structural or semantic. She clasps her hands and thrusts her index fingers forward like she's aiming her rifle.

"Mistakes were made," she says. "But changes come."

The Mother finds Bristol in the bathroom, hunched over the toilet.

The Mother extends her hand. Bristol clasps it and finds it warm and pulsing. The Mother separates the fingers of her other hand and gently strokes Bristol's hair.

"Hold on," the Mother says. "Hold on as long as you can."

House Party

Boy Who Is Evan, and Loves Stephen

.....

Dearest Stephen,

I think I'm in love with you.

There. I said it. I guess it wasn't that hard. My best friend Kandace and I have a competition. Her boyfriend drives a Plymouth, and you drive a used Mercedes. So whenever she spots a Plymouth, she gets one point, and whenever I spot a Mercedes, I get one. I'm usually in the lead. But I didn't mean to imply you were my boyfriend. How embarrassing.

I should start over. I'm writing because you won't see me for a while, and I want you to know why. My mother says my stepdad and I never pitch in around the house. She says nobody considers her needs, how she's overextended at work and has incompetent support staff. A pile of papers, cereal boxes and CDs has been sitting on our dining room table for over a month, and she says it's all our fault, my stepdad's and mine.

My report card came the other day. You know how I go to that fruity progressive school where they send personalized comments? Well my grades were okay, but my teachers called me flighty and distant. Now my mother says I lied when I said everything was great, and how can she love me if she can't trust me? Also because this was my junior year, which they say is the most important for applying to college. I cannot tell her it was because of you I left class and wandered through the hallways daydreaming. So now I have to spend the entire summer organizing our garage.

Do you remember the night we met at Holly's birthday party? We were outside, you and me and Holly, singing songs from musicals, and I said I was cold, and you offered me your jacket. It was an actual, for-real letter jacket, like the ones on teen soap operas. Going to high school in the city, I'm unaccustomed to seeing such things in real life. For a second, I felt more comfortable around you than anyone I'd ever met. Then I took another look at your impossibly yellow hair and the tan you probably got skiing or yachting, and I heard the lilt in your voice, and realized you might indeed share my proclivities, and my stomach abandoned me. I grew self-conscious and withdrew into your letter jacket, speaking the words to the songs from musicals instead of singing them, as though I were Rex Harrison.

Holly says you talk about me when I'm not around. You ask, "How's Evan?" and "When's Evan coming to visit?" Holly says even the girl you're dating knows my name because you're always talking about me.

But then whenever I call you, you ask whether I've met anybody nice, and I worry, what if you're sending me a message to move on?

Oh, that's the other reason my mother's mad. She found out about the calls to you I charged to her calling card while we were on vacation. So in addition to cleaning the garage, I'm supposed to get a job and pay back every penny. But I'm afraid to ask for applications.

All of which is to say I'll be out of touch for a while. In the meantime, I need to know once and for all whether you feel the same. Even if I don't like the answer, although I hope you will share my feelings, because I believe we were destined for something extraordinary.

I won't be able to answer the phone if you call me, but I can usually sneak into my stepdad's study to check my email. So please, email your response. Until then, I will wait, breathlessly and lovingly yours,

Evan

Grace

Boy Who Loves Kevin

.....

Our counselor Kevin opened his guitar case. The case was battered and road-weary, but the guitar itself—a pearl! It glistened like Kevin himself, buffed and boffed. He had recently graduated, was applying to seminaries, which seemed a formality. I knew he was already as close to God as any human being could possibly get.

We kept journals of our travels through Guatemala. We set time aside each morning for reflection. Where did you see Christ in Champerico? What acts has God called us to perform? I scratched Kevin's name in repetition. Kevin, Kevin, Kevin, Kevin. Play me your guitar. Sing me into heaven.

In Puerto Barrios, we rebuilt a church destroyed by flooding. I watched Kevin, how his wet white tank clung to his chest, how his shoulders rippled and dimpled and shook when he lifted weight, and I'd sneak into the Porta-Potty to jack off.

We visited a maquila skirted by an electric fence. I wanted Kevin to press me against it, to feel charges pulse me from ahead and behind.

I'd pass beneath the high, open window when Kevin showered and imagine him inside, picture thighs, penis, steam.

At night, my stomach raged. Food didn't stay put, for a week I was laid down. I imagined myself sick with longing.

On the shelf above my bed, I unpacked, positioned, displayed my books, everything I thought Kevin could appreciate—texts on liberation theology, my New Revised Standard Bible, albums by Bruce Cockburn.

I drew in my journal. Kevin, one arm around the guitar and the other around me. I thought this was all I ever wanted to be, an instrument he used to communicate his soul. I imagined my insides flushed with Kevin, flushed with the Holy Spirit. In church bulletins, the Spirit was a dove, but I knew it was a song, a song Kevin sang, and whenever he sang, I knew the Spirit came inside me.

I thought about how the village flooded, how the waters rose to cover and destroy. I thought about how this brought us here, brought Kevin into my life and thought maybe God really did have a plan. No no no, I do not mean this as selfishly as it sounds. I meant we'd bring change, become instruments of God's grace. Together.

My friend Rachel began to wonder why I ignored her, grew jealous. She glanced over my shoulder during our morning journaling and I shrugged her off. He's straight, you moron, she said. He'll never love you. Think about Christ, I said. There are other kinds of love. Maybe that would be enough.

It wasn't. I followed him on his walk down to the river to swim. I hid in the undergrowth and watched him peel away his layers—Dear God! I pulled it out and wanked, watching him. Just before I came I heard him coming near—I must have rustled the reeds—and as his mouth closed around me, I felt the spread of grace.

House of Wax

Boy Who Is Evan, Crashing with Kandace

.....

I've been crashing on Kandace's couch for a week when she finally asks why my mother kicked me out. We're sitting on Kandace's fire escape and watching the sunset when she asks.

"It started with the wax," I say.

"The wax?" she says.

"It happened a few weeks after I came home for the summer. My mom and my stepdad were away for the weekend. The first night they were gone, I lit all these candles and drank a full bottle of wine and twirled around the living room in my bathrobe humming along to *New York Tendaberry*."

Kandace frowns. I have always had a bad habit of dropping references I know no one around me will understand.

"Laura Nyro?"

Kandace shook her head.

"Anyway, I fall asleep on the couch, because of all that wine. And then the candles burn down to their ends, and wax spills all over the floor and my mother's furniture. Most of her pieces are solid oak antiques my grandmother bought her at auction.

"I wake up the next morning and there's all this wax everywhere. But I've still got two more days before my parents come home, so I tell myself I'll take care of it later, and I walk downtown to catch a movie. Well two days pass and I still haven't taken care of it. My parents are on their way home, and I panic. I start trying to take off the wax with a knife, all frantic, and my mother walks in the door just in time to see me dig a gouge out of her favorite side table.

"She was furious. She made me call a refinishing company to get an estimate. She said I had to pay for it. She said because I hadn't shown any respect for her possessions, I wasn't allowed to take her extra laptop to school next year, and I'd have to go to the computer lab to write my papers. She said she wasn't going to give me any money for textbooks, I'd have to earn it all myself. And then I spent weeks cleaning wax off the furniture. I even tried that Martha Stewart trick with the iron."

"Oh," Kandace says. A car alarm blares in a nearby alley. A woman in an adjacent building hangs her laundry out to dry.

"So your mother kicked you out because you ruined her furniture?" Kandace says.

"No," I say. "She kicked me out because of the letter from my college."

"Letter?" Kandace says, when she realizes I'm not going to elaborate.

"They requested I take a year off due to my poor performance," I say. "I was scraping wax off the sideboard when my mother came into the living room holding the letter. She said I lied to her. She said my lies were abusive. She said I was causing her more pain than I caused during childbirth. Then she said what I'd done was no different than what my father did. She said it felt like I'd hit her, just like my father. She said she wanted me out of the house by the next day."

"Wow," Kandace says.

"The weird thing is," I say. "She used to make threats like that all the time. She used to tell me she was going to send me to live with my father. She'd say she was going to force me to leave private school and send me back to public school, where I used to get beat up. And I knew she didn't mean it, I knew she would take it all back later and tell me my real punishment, but I still believed her. Every time, I believed her.

"But this time, I was perfectly calm. I took her at her word. I packed my bags and left that very night, while she and my stepdad went out to a diner to decompress."

"I know what you mean," Kandace says. "I felt that way when I left my mother's house. Perfectly calm."

I remember this. We were in high school. Kandace got into an argument with her mother and her mother sat on her face. Then she pushed her out the front door and locked her outside without any shoes. Kandace had to walk twenty blocks to the nearest police station.

She moved in with her father the next day. Kandace worships her father.

"Right," I say. "Perfectly calm."

"Exactly," Kandace says. "Calm."

We huddle together on the fire escape. Kandace drops her ear against my shoulder. The sun sets in panoramic Technicolor, and we sit watching, perfectly calm.

Marionette

Boy Who Steals Soda

.....

When I wake up in the morning, my sheets are sweaty, and the last thing I want to think about is going to class. If I close my eyes tight enough, I can force myself back to sleep.

I've got an email from this guy who lives a few blocks from campus and works at the medical center. He wants to meet me.

It's dark outside when I go. It's been a while since I've seen the campus during daylight. Lately whenever I cross the street I think I'm going to get hit by a car. Decapitation is what I think about. My neck seems so thin anymore. I wrap my hands around it and say, "Stay, head. Stay on." But probably if I got hit by a car, I wouldn't get decapitated, I don't think that actually happens.

I get to his house and he shows me around. This is my favorite part of sex, when people take me home or let me in. I like to watch them get ready for me, take my coat and fix me something to drink.

I lie on the bed and I throw up my legs and he puts on a condom and pushes inside me, but he can't keep it up for very long.

"I'm sorry," he says, and rolls over on his back. "I'm a little preoccupied. A boy died on the table today."

He wants a confidant, I think. This I can do. In high school my friends called me a good listener.

"I'm so sorry," I say, and rub his belly like a troll doll.

He smacks my hand away, pushes me, and I roll to the edge of the bed. It kind of hurts.

"I'm sorry," he says. "I shouldn't have done that."

"I understand," I say. "My father's a surgeon."

No he isn't.

"I could move in here, you know," I say. "I can clean things, and I cook too. I think you need somebody to talk to, and I don't have much stuff."

"You should go," he says.

"Call me?"

Walking back through campus, I look at the terracotta roofs and think I should climb on top of one, dance, crush the tiles. That would attract some attention.

When I decided to come here for school, what I thought I'd do was stay up all night talking about theories. Like I have this theory because everything is interconnected, if we learn to use our brains right, we could become everything everywhere at once. Or maybe just one thing in particular, but totally different from whatever we are right now. My friends and I have stayed up a couple of times, but all they wanted to do was drink and watch porn and talk about their favorite actors.

I kind of want a Pepsi, but my meal card is cashed, so I go into the late night student pub and I do this thing where I grab the soda from the case while the lunch lady isn't looking. I stick the bottle inside my jacket and run. I'm on my way out when I hear the lunch lady say, "Stop!" But I keep on running away.

Housekeeping

Boy Who Is Not a Boy, but Evan's Mother

.....

The burners on the stovetop are never clean. They are caked with sauces, with stray bits of food, and the responsibility for cleaning falls to me alone. This problem was worse when Evan lived here, but it has continued long after. I tell my husband Randall I'd appreciate him cleaning up after himself. I tell him this in his own language, the language of a psychotherapist.

"When you leave food on the stovetop," I tell him. "I feel you disrespect my labor."

"Your frustration is valid," Randall says, trained as he is to diffuse conflict. "I will do better."

Days later, food still sticks to the burners and I'm forced to attack the problem with scouring powder and an abrasive sponge.

Just visible out of the corner of my eye sits the kitchen table where Evan first told us he was homosexual, by writing it on a piece of paper he handed us during dinner. His announcement came as no surprise. I'd anticipated it since Evan was a small child, and had worked to provide him with respectable gay role models, friends and colleagues I knew would assist him as he wrestled with his identity.

The note he wrote us said, "I think I'm gay." Randall, whose own son is ten years older than Evan and lives with his partner in Brooklyn, pumped his fists and said, "Yes! I have two gay sons!" I glared, pursed my lips and said, "That's not what this note says."

Evan used to tell me it was my duty to be proud of him. As a parent, I'd tell him, it was more important I model honesty. While I consider myself an advocate of civil rights for gays and lesbians, I cannot lie by telling Evan I'm happy he's who he is. I worry for his safety, just as I'd worry for the safety of a daughter, if I had one. Men do not respect boundaries. Men lie.

When Evan was a child, perhaps six or seven years old, he rode beside me as I drove to a weekend work obligation. After a week of eight-hour workdays and long meetings, I felt fatigued. At a stoplight, I placed my head to the steering wheel and said, "I'm just a little old lady."

"Mommy," Evan said. "You're not little."

I laughed. And then I laughed some more. Then Evan laughed. And I laughed again. And we laughed together, laughing at our own laughter.

I think about that a lot lately.

Unnecessary

Boy Who Has a Batty Mother

.....

I reached my mother's doorstep with an important message, written in advance and practiced in front of a mirror. She answered in a purple kimono, her lips and cheeks rouged. She stretched across the doorframe, steel-eyed and implacable.

"I balanced my checkbook," I told her. "I wanted to tell you. I've been recording all my purchases in my register. I'm adding and subtracting."

She arched her brow.

"But I suspect even this will not be enough for you. You will expect more, you will expect me to categorize these expenses, assign colors and make pie charts. You set unreachable expectations because you want me to fail you, because then you remain necessary. Well I'm here to tell you–you are not necessary. I love you, but you are not necessary."

"Come in," my mother said, extending the storm door. "Your sister will want to see you."

"My sister?"

In the foyer, a tiny blond tornado whirled by.

"Say hello to your brother," my mother said.

"Hello," she said. Her skin was pale, her cheeks patched with red. She looked maybe six years old.

"She must be a great deal taller than the last time you saw her?"

I said, "I do not have a sister."

"Of course," my mother said. "I'd forgotten. Your sister must not have been around much when you were growing up. The demands of one child are overwhelming enough, and you were an especially demanding child. Still, it's rather cruel to deny her existence, wouldn't you say?"

"I do not have a sister," I repeated.

"I will make us some hot chocolate," my mother said.

I sat on the couch and watched the small blond girl yank plush squirrels from a columnar tree trunk sewn from fabric scraps. The squirrels were stuffed with tiny horns that squeaked. These were my Woodsy family. The small blond girl was playing with my Woodsies.

She lined up the Woodsies in a row. She said, "They're going to the opera. They're going to see *Das Rheingold*."

They're squirrels, I thought. They can't go to the opera. There's no opera in the forest.

"A new flavor," my mother said, wielding a tray of steaming mugs. "Dulce de leche. White chocolate with caramel."

"I have to poop," said the small blond girl, and disappeared into the hallway.

I sipped.

"Did you take a six-year-old girl to see Wagner?" I said.

The small blond girl came back and reached for a mug.

"Did you wash your hands?" said my mother, holding back the tray.

The small blond girl shook her head, shame-faced, and turned in the other direction.

"Make sure you count to fifty," my mother called behind her.

"They say twenty seconds," she said, addressing me. "But young children count quickly."

Later, on my way out the door, my mother placed her hand on my upper back.

"I'm glad you're finally taking care of yourself, darling," she said. "But I will always be necessary."

The Cider House Rules

Boy Who Is Patrick, Evan's Boyfriend

.....

Here's what nobody understands. I'm not judgmental. When I call my boyfriend's behavior destructive, I'm not judging. It's not about good or bad or right or wrong. It's about Evan destroying something. He's destroying himself and our relationship. I fail to understand the appeal of putting one's life at risk for the sake of fun. How much fun can he be having if he doesn't remember anything?

So tonight I made him promise. I made him tell me how many drinks he would drink and what time he'd be home. Evan says he believes in harm reduction, that abstinence is a setup for failure, but that he can create mechanisms to reduce the potential for harm. I ask him what kind of mechanisms, and he says, "I'll set limits."

I met Evan five-and-a-half years ago, at the bar he tends. Evan is 14 years younger than me. This isn't my first relationship with a younger man. I know I can depend on certain things and not on others. Cash flow, for instance. But younger men will always need you. Until they stop needing you. And then all you have left are files full of lovelorn emails and photo albums of vacations abroad.

I am frequently disappointed by Evan. It's not that I have some litmus test for the ideal relationship, and Evan fails to measure up. It's more that I see wasted potential in the nuanced theories he details to barflies, or the poems he scrawls on napkins. Evan says it's too late to be special, so he'll settle for remaining calm. Evan is 28 years old.

I'm already in bed when Evan stumbles through the door, two hours past our agreed-upon time.

"Sorry," he says. "Sorry."

In the dark, I can just barely make him out.

"How many drinks did you have?" I say.

"I'm fine," he says. He raises his voice and enunciates the word fine.

"How many drinks did you have?" I say.

"Three ciders," he says. "Like I promised."

"You're lying," I say. "I can hear it in your voice."

"I'm fine," he says.

I flick on the lamp on our bedside table.

Evan's lower lip is split, busted open. Blood cakes beneath his mouth and above his chin.

"What happened?" I say.

"Doan' remember," he says.

I feel terrified and angry, unsure whether to punch Evan or embrace him. So I do the only thing I know how to do. I grab a washcloth from the linen closet and wet it with warm water. I sit Evan on the bed. As I clutch his shoulder with one hand and dab the blood from his face with the other, I think maybe this is love. Maybe love is holding another person's potential when they're too weak to hold it themselves.

Loaded

Boy Who Flips His Shit

.....

Sometimes I remember all the reasons I shouldn't own a gun. Like the other day when a man in an SUV cut me off as I crossed the street, and I wanted to block his vehicle, tear open the driver's side door, kick the door off its hinge, yank out the driver by his shirt collar, jam the heel of my boot into the center of his face, dig out his eyes with my fingertips, stuff his eyes into his mouth until he gagged, then twist his arms like screw tops until they popped off at the shoulder, then bend him over the hood, pull down his slacks and fist him with his own hand, all the while screaming, "Pedestrian motherfucking right of way, you fuckhead, pedestrian motherfucking right of way." This would not have been a good time to carry a firearm.

Or the time at the airport subway stop, when the fare card vending machine wouldn't accept my bills, and I was toting heavy suitcases, and the train began to announce its departure, so I balled my fist and hammered the machine, hoping it would dent, hoping it would burst open, and a stooped, crotchety transit employee came out of his bulletproof booth to say, "Sir, don't punch the machine," and I said, "Maybe the transit authority should get some fucking machines that work," and then the tamper alarm sounded, and the crotchety employee said, "That's it! Now you're going to jail," and officers came and cuffed me and drove me to the nearest precinct in a paddywagon, and my lover had to come from his precinct, the one where he works as a detective, to bail me out, which he almost didn't do, in order to teach me a lesson, and when we got home, he said, "You are going to tell me how you plan to confront your anger, or you are going to lose this relationship."

When I was in middle school, other boys called me a faggot, which is perhaps unsurprising, but do you remember what it feels like to be called a faggot? It isn't just something people say. They were sophisticated readers of popular culture, those middle school boys. This was back when they aired that Diet Coke commercial, the one with the shirtless construction worker with sweat-beaded pectorals, who popped his can top in synchronization with my erection. "Diet Coke break," the boys hounded me. "Diet Coke break!" And once, I lifted my desk and threw it at these boys as far as I could throw, which wasn't very far, and I flailed my arms and kicked my legs, and my classmates had to restrain me.

Like I imagine my lover restrains criminals who resist arrest. I watch my lover holster his gun before he leaves the house each morning. I would never lift a hand against my lover, but sometimes, when we have sex, if I am feeling less than fully "in the moment" and if his body feels to me assaultive, I squeeze his arms with excessive force, and must apologize and attribute my forcefulness to arousal, and then I wonder what would happen if I punched him below his nose, above his jaw, I wonder, if I punched him, how much he would bleed.

Fugitives

Boy Who Thinks He Isn't the Fugitive

.....

Most nights, Calvin and I lie in bed and watch TV. Calvin's stomach is a pillow, but I don't mind. Calvin flips the channels. With each channel flipped, sound explodes. "Will you stop?" I say. "You're making me epileptic." Calvin grabs my cock and says, "Do I make you seize?" I kiss him on the mouth.

On the 10:00 news, the announcer says, "police have surrounded the home of the couple they believe to be harboring the fugitive." A phalanx of cop cars circles the house. From the chopper, the house looks like a tiny blue box. It looks like cardboard. I want to crush it with my boot. It looks familiar.

"That's our house," Calvin says.

"Open the door," a voice booms through a megaphone. "Allow us to inspect your property."

We don bathrobes, gray and taupe, and tiptoe to the door. I feel euphoric, like I want to get hard, and I wonder whether the policeman will talk dirty through the megaphone.

"We know you're in there."

Lately, I have often felt as though Calvin is hiding something. For instance, the other evening, when I arrived home from work, I found he'd cooked pork tenderloin for dinner. Sliced meat glittered on plates, luminous, white and threatening. Why pork tenderloin, I wondered, and why that night? I look at him, to see if his eyes will answer me, but instead I see the panicked expression of a person reconsidering everything. He thinks it's me.

"Will you leave us alone?" Calvin says. "It's almost bedtime and your lights are distracting."

"Hand over the fugitive and no harm will come to you."

Calvin looks at me. He looks at the living room. He says, "There's no one here I'd call a fugitive."

"If there's no fugitive, you have nothing to lose by opening the door."

The policeman butts in, all jackboots, buckles and chrome. He twirls a big stick and points. He orders us to empty our cabinets and we line up cereal boxes on the countertop: Cocoa Puffs, Lucky Charms, Bamm-Bamm Berry Pebbles. We gather items from our nightstand: Lubricant, condoms, a vibrating butt plug. The policeman opens the closet and rifles through rows of Calvin's suits. He yanks them from the rack, piles them on the floor, a lopsided mound of navy, brown and black. He fondles the television remote and snickers as he inspects the season passes in our DVR. He turns on his heels and marches toward the door.

"Wait," Calvin calls. "Are we cleared?"

The policeman stops. He watches us, reconsiders us, our life, our habits, our stuff.

"It was a mistake," Calvin says. "Tell us it was a mistake."

The policeman jams the door behind him.

"He didn't tell us," Calvin says. "Tell us it was a mistake."

Life as a House

Boy Who Is Not a Boy, but Evan's House

.....

When Evan first lived here with his mother, I used to listen to her read him *The Giving Tree*.

Do you know the story of the Giving Tree? It's about a boy who becomes best friends with a tree. Across the course of his life, he uses the tree. For shelter, recreation, to build a boat.

I have always loved this story. I identify with the tree. I suppose it will come as no surprise that life as a house resembles life as the Giving Tree. I would give my very timbers to protect the family inside me.

As a house, certain things are beyond your control. You cannot, for instance, cure illness. You can only function like the drugs, providing comfort and managing the end. When Evan's mother got sick, her ex-husband Randall called to tell him. Evan moved back and brought his lover Patrick. And although he agrees to read his mother *The Giving Tree*, I've heard him denouncing my favorite story.

"Classic Christian bullshit," he said one night, curled against Patrick in his mother's antique four-poster. "Give and give and give and give, think nothing of yourself, until you're nothing but a stump. And then some crusty codger sticks his ass in your face."

"But my mother's always loved it," he said. "No wonder she was such a basket case."

People who are not objects cannot possibly understand. When you are an object, all you can do is give. Otherwise, you sit, doing nothing.

Evan and his mother play board games, watch musicals and reminiscence, carefully avoiding any mention of the decade they didn't speak. Evan opens *The Giving Tree*, reads "You may cut off my branches and build a house. Then you will be happy."

What if the Dungeon Closes

Boy Who Hangs with a Dominatrix

.....

This was around the time when all the restaurants started closing. We'd go out to dinner and find our first choice padlocked, windows white-washed, chairs balanced treacherously on tables. When we got to our second choice, our third choice, our fourth choice, it'd be packed. No one was spending any money, yet everyone went out to eat. And for the restaurant lucky enough to secure their patronage, a stay of execution.

"I feel terrible for all my friends who are losing their jobs," Marlena said, crunching her salad. "It's like the bottom's falling out. People are falling, hanging from the sides of buildings screaming 'help! help!' like in those cartoons from when we were kids."

I nodded. I was tired of this conversation about cartoons from the 1980s.

"It's times like these I'm glad I left corporate America."

Marlena was a professional dom. Men paid her to whip and insult them. She was always telling me how much less exploited she felt than when she'd worked as an administrative assistant.

"You feel like your job is secure?" I asked.

"Most of the time," she said. "But then we'll have a day with fewer clients, and I'll start to worry... I mean what if the Dungeon closes? What would I do then?"

I pictured an iron grate crashing, locking. I thought about Marlena's clients, lonely men, wondered how they'd get by. They'd listen to stale, recorded insults in cramped apartments. They'd whip their own asses, dissatisfied because they always knew exactly where the whip would land. This reminded me of myself trolling internet sex sites, firing five-word missives to Adonises carved from clay, then grabbing my sagging stomach and thinking better of it, erasing my messages, erasing my profile, creating a new one the following day.

It was dark outside when Marlena and I left the restaurant. Winter was coming, the sun set early. Marlena threaded her arm through mine and walked me home.

About the Author

.....

Tim Jones-Yelvington has been called the Lady Gaga of the Chicago lit scene. His work has appeared or is forthcoming in *Another Chicago Magazine*, *Sleepingfish*, *Annalemma*, and many others. He has guest edited for *Pank* and *Smokelong Quarterly*, and serves as the President of the Board of Directors of *Artifice Magazine*. His website is timjonesyelvington.com.

How Some People Like Their Eggs

::::: *Sean Lovelace* :::::

Acknowledgments

"Meteorite" *Puerto del Sol*

"Charlie Brown's Diary: Excerpts" *Keyhole Magazine* online

"I Love Bocce" *New Orleans Review*

"A Sigh Is Just a Sigh" *Wigleaf*

"Wal-Mart" *Puerto del Sol*

"Coffee Pot Tree" *River Styx*

"Endings" *flashquake* online

Table of Contents

Meteorite

.....

The only recorded meteorite to actually hit a human being sits in a glass case on the second floor of Smith Hall, the University of Alabama's museum of natural history. The meteorite hit a woman with hair wrapped high like a hornet's nest, in the left thigh. There's a photo in the glass case. The woman stands on her front steps, hip-handed, clearly not smiling. It makes me think of god and lack of god and luck—good, bad, out of, etc.—and this newspaper story I read last summer about a Good Samaritan who pulled over on the highway to help change a woman's tire and was struck dead by a semi. I think of that exhausted word, *destiny*.

My friend Paige and I walk past Smith Hall. We are walking, long, aimless walking, like two paper cups blown across a grassy courtyard. Paige spent nine hours yesterday in a teal gown sitting on a cold table. Her ass was often exposed. A nurse took her blood, missing her vein and leaving a bruise in the crook of her arm in the shape of Hawaii's largest island, Hawaii. A doctor told Paige she had leukemia, a disease wherein the white cells run amuck and drink too much cheap beer and urinate in public and hang from motel balconies and generally harm themselves and others like teenagers on spring break in Florida.

We sit on the patio of a restaurant that serves college kids, and very bad food. It is expensive and comes in tiny portions and leaves a bland, greasy film across your teeth, all of it. I once thought bar food was impossible to ruin, since it is generally dropped into a deep fat fryer and served with plastic cups of ketchup. I was wrong.

Paige and I don't order food, only tall beers, the bubbles rising like glass elevators. An ambulance drives by slowly, its bells and whistles asleep. It waddles into a parking spot. Two fat paramedics get out and go inside to eat bad bar food. I think of Paige and me drifting off somewhere in glass elevators but the image doesn't catch and two sorority girls stroll by looking absolutely themselves.

I wonder what I should say to Paige.

I try, "I guess it'll be rough for a while."

I try, "You can always use my car, you know, for appointments or whatever. I could pick you up."

I try, "It doesn't really mean what it used to, right? I mean, they got treatments."

I try silence.

Silence works, and eventually Paige pulls a crumpled ball of pamphlets from the pocket of her jeans. She slides the wadded ball across the table and the wind blows it to the ground and I trap two of the pamphlets with my foot. One of the pamphlets has photographs of models wearing wigs. The other is entitled: "The Ten Commandments for Cancer Survival."

Seriously.

Commandment # 2: "Thou shalt love thy chemotherapy, thy radiation, and thy other treatments even as thyself, for they are thy friends and champions."

Commandment # 9: "Thou shalt maintain, at all times and in all circumstances, thy sense of humor, for laughter lightens thy heart and hastens thy recovery."

I hand Paige the pamphlets, their glossy pages leaving my grip like pin-pulled grenades. She folds them into her empty beer glass and waves the waitress over. Paige orders bar food. She orders nachos and Buffalo wings and fried calamari and two baskets of cheese sticks and a thing called Triple Play, a platter of fried jalapeño poppers, French fries, and onion rings.

Plastic cups of ketchup sprout like mushrooms on the dried manure disk of our patio table. Paige eats everything and says her stomach kind of hurts and I say I bet it kind of hurts. She says I'd win that bet and then orders the entire dessert menu, including an ice cream pie called Chocolate to Die For.

Commandment # 9 . . .

Two years later I spent my spring break in a small Florida town where you could simply pitch your tent on the beach and lift sand dollars off the ocean bottom like lost Frisbees and see so many stars at night it was stupid.

Charlie Brown's Diary: Excerpts

.....

Tuesday, February 14, 1958: I wake, and hear the birds coughing. Some dog barking. My coal-smudge eyes sting with sleep. In a hotel near a train station, yawning off Löwenbräu fumes in my zig-zag shirt. Or maybe I lie. Maybe just my yellow room. My parents call, but all I hear is breath and breathing, muffled pipes, misunderstandings—another day stripped, routine as the rain. I've come to believe all adults are lost. I swear to God in 1954 I won a bowling trophy. And a free haircut, for my two scraggly hairs. My father is a barber. Why do you play my name, Maker? Blockhead? My head is round, and full of etchings.

Tuesday, March 2, 1969: I wake, and hear the birds coughing. Snoopy flies in today. His goggles scratched, one ear torn and bleeding, but his eyes aglow. "Sex underwater is overrated," he says dryly. "Too much friction." I have no reply. It all adds to my notion: there is a bigger world, outside of mine. *Where is the doorway?* I want to ask

Snoopy. *Show me the way, before it's too late.* But he just stands there, opening and closing a silver Zippo, gazing out the window, already far away. The air is filled with sea salt, butane, a hint of almonds, an aroma that lingers for days.

Tuesday, May 9, 1971: I wake, and hear the birds coughing. Under the night blanket. I do the math, in the bowl of my head, and I am not going to lie. Two wins, 930 losses. My responsibility. My team. Starting pitcher, manager—that's me. Two wins. The two games I missed, in January, that long weekend on the ninth floor.

Tuesday, November 4, 1975: I wake, and hear the birds coughing. Sunlight through the window like a train. I took a trip once, to Kansas. I ate fried steak and visited strip clubs and drank myself silly on three-dollar truck-stop mojitos. I cavorted with red-haired whores. All of this yesterday, or in some lost panel. Waking is a dull ache. Most of me is onionskin. Yesterday I flew a kite, into a waterfall. Yesterday I was invisible. Or was that Chuck?

Tuesday, March 14, 1984: I wake, and hear the birds coughing. Seven, fourteen, twenty-eight times—the phone rings. It's Franklin: Did I hear? Schroeder bought an Acura MDX. What does that mean? Why is everything an *x, y…z*? All these medications. Spaceship names. Shapes and colors. They want to lift me and soar away. This same musty shirt, 34 years. One dog bowl. One stubby pencil. Drawn. Drawn is my word.

Tuesday, April 2, 2000: I wake, and hear the birds coughing. I can't arise today. Twenty sudden pounds. Sandpaper mouth, itchy head. My thoughts are growing smaller. A doghouse echo. Soggy blanket. Something gnawed. At least the sun is shining. I see a sliver of light, a patch of emerald lawn. My perfectly square window, dusty pane. *Good grief.* An oxymoron, or maybe life. Four panels. And here comes Lucy, so briskly; she seems to float...she's holding a football.

I Love Bocce

.....

There was a time I thought most everyone should play bocce. I was like Rico Daniele, author of *Bocce: A Sport For Everyone* and president of the Wonderful World of Bocce Association, who would say to anyone, "Let's get bocce courts in schools and playgrounds for the kids, parents, and grandparents."

I wasn't well.

I was in nursing school and that was plenty. I had an unrequited crush on a girl named Lilly. I had a chronically sore Achilles heel and couldn't exercise.

Overall, I was slightly depressed.

This is what the university therapist said:

"You're confusing your feelings for a young lady with the game she introduced you to. It's classic transference."

"You have to let it go."

"I'm not one of those New York shrinks with a fancy office."

"Everything isn't about bocce."

Of course, everything wasn't about bocce. But tell that to my world.

Example, the very next day:

My OR rotation and we were standing around a blue-mummied patient with a defunct gallbladder. There was the head surgeon and me and my nursing instructor and a medical student and a circulating nurse with long, stringy hair—like something out of a clogged drain, etc.—and a scrub nurse and a nurse anesthetist with a sad smile.

My instructor and I were only observing. We'd been going about an hour, routine stuff, clamp this, cut here, watch that bleeder, and so on, when the head surgeon yelled out, "Anyone here like bocce?"

I started, and sweat popped up on my forehead.

"I dated an Italian guy who was crazy about it," the circulating nurse said, following the surgeon's lead. "Liked bocce so much he would shoot the balls out of a replica cannon, or store them in the refrigerator fruit drawer. Sometimes, he'd swallow the balls, and, well . . .wait."

"That's what I mean," the surgeon said, as he sutured a neat bow over a vein. "Dedication. Extractor."

Handing over the extractor, the scrub nurse added, "I once played a round with inflatable bocce balls, inflated with helium, at a side show in Indiana."

"I like bocce as well as anyone," the medical student said. He followed the surgeon's fingers as they lifted a lung. "I once drove a convertible bocce ball cross country."

Everyone ignored the student. He was trying to impress the surgeon.

The nurse anesthetist sighed and said, "The last man off a bocce field rarely looks back."

Everyone nodded his or her head. I felt like a cloud in someone else's dream.

"Has anyone seen a snake that's eaten a bocce ball?" said the surgeon. "Suction." He stood away as the scrub nurse cleared the surgical field, then continued. "I did once. In Africa. I was up 13-4 on a group of native chaps—Masabis or whatnot—and a cobra snatched my ball, of course couldn't digest it." He paused and snipped away a layer of fascia. No one answered him. Surgeons were always assuming everyone routinely traveled to Africa.

"I played in Haiti," the medical student said, "with coconuts, during a tournament. I actually grouped the balls so close that several laws of physics were altered."

No answer. The Pulsox beeped; someone paged someone over the intercom.

Finally, the nurse anesthetist offered, "I play decent bocce when dreaming, or just unconscious. Compared to unconscious, my conscious bocce is nothing."

The surgeon grunted. "Now," he said, "I'm sure your conscious bocce is something, too."

"Not at all," the nurse anesthetist said, reaching up to adjust the drip on an IV.

All this talk about bocce, I felt I was going to faint. I felt normal.

"I love bocce," I blurted out, and everyone turned to stare at me. The surgeon frowned, eyed my instructor, and said, "Let's close this up."

Later, my instructor wrote me up for unprofessional behavior. To top it off she passed me a tiny bottle of Scope and said my breath smelled like pizza. I think it was pizza, but she may have said ravioli.

It was a while ago.

I wasn't well.

A Sigh Is Just a Sigh

.....

My Wife

claimed no one ever said "Play it again, Sam" in the movie *Casablanca.*

I told her no way that was true. No way are all these people going around, quoting that line, cherishing that line, claiming that line as theirs—and then it never existed at all.

"Look it up," she said flatly, and returned to the Scrabble board.

Ingrid Bergman

told me she'd sleep with any man who desired. And there had been plenty. She slept with the majority of her costars on every film, most of the directors, several costume designers, and once, for kicks, a sound-effects editor—"helps me get into the role," she argued. It didn't bother her at all. It was like taking a walk, "like reading from a script," she said.

I was tempted. Oh god, I was tempted. Things like that don't just fall into your lap, and, honestly, my blood thrummed with the possibility. To put it plainly, it had been a while. But no, I told her, I just couldn't.

She said, "You ever seen a Nordic woman naked? Skin like fresh milk..."

She said, "I'm more flexible than I might appear, I'll tell you that."

She said, "Are you jesting? Marriage? That's just the art of saying no."

She said, "Do you mind if I smoke? Do you mind if I place this cigarette between my moist lips, and set it on fire?"

I told her actually I did mind. No tobacco smoke in the house, please.

She popped open her Zippo, lit, and inhaled. Blew a thin tunnel-cloud into my ceiling fan. Said, "Well then, come over here and stop me."

Later that evening my wife said she smelled something in the house. Those exact words: "I-smell-something."

"Ok," I said, and walked outside, to winterize the lawn.

The Doorbell

rang. I suffer some strange phobia concerning visitors to the front door, so whispered up to the peephole: a tall man, in a dull gray military uniform, cap, belt, holster, what appeared to be a pistol.

"Choose!" he said loudly. "You must choose: a trick, or a treat."

I stood in silence, holding my breath.

"Attention! I am selling *National Geographic* subscription and decorative candles. For a youth group. What kind of man would deny himself a glimpse at a larger world, and an instrument to light the way?" He shifted in the warming sunlight, took off his cap, scratched his head.

In the bedroom, the droning of water, my wife showering. She was running late for a business trip to Fort Wayne, Indiana.

The man re-rang the doorbell, and stood there, blinking. His voice cracking a bit, he said, "Please open this door. I found your little dog. Your little dog was running free, over the hills and the roadways. Now I return him, so you can rope or chain him to your home, whatever is your pleasure. He will wag his tail. Don't you want to see him wag his tail, and call him happy?"

Strange, how time can bend and stretch. Minutes into hours, and so on. The shower faded, and a toilet flushed.

"Oh, you!" the man said, his face reddening. His hand dropped to his holster, and my pulse kicked up. But then he paused, and shouted, "Oh you of very bad faith!"

Like a child, he made a face at the doorway, a scrunched-up scowl, then turned on his heels, marched up the street, and was gone.

Humphrey Bogart

woke fully clothed in the guest room and complained about my futon: "Got a metal bar running down the middle. Hurts my back."

Actually, my futon frame was made of cedar. And had eight inches of mattress foam. The industry standard is six inches. I paid extra. I didn't tell him any of this. I just said, "You want some Pop-Tarts or something?"

He gave me this look. "You see this face?" he said. "How do I get by with this face? Looks like a potato."

I suggested many found his face handsome, in a rugged way.

He coughed, a dry rasping, and dug in his shirt pocket for a pack of Chesterfields. He said, "You don't know squat, do you? But thanks for the bunk. My wife is crazy. She'll be home right now with a knife, or a gun. She has one. But a man needs to face what he's made for himself, kid. I hope you're learning something here. I hope you're watching."

I was watching. He lit a cigarette, and I said nothing. A siren rose and fell in the distance. Or maybe the howl of a neighbor's dog. Bogart rocked himself up from the futon, and stood wincing. Rubbed his left knee and said, "Ever had your kneecap broken?"

I said I hadn't.

"Well, you will, one day. Sure as the rain. And you'll touch that place your whole life."

I rolled the garbage out on a Tuesday evening. A gigantic moon: silver and crackling. The bin caught the curb edge and toppled over. Overfull as usual: Bisquick, a bag of stale croutons, empty bottles of

Zinfandel, and a coffee maker. We bought a new coffee maker, one with pause-and-serve, and I had no idea what to do with the old one. I was thinking how—

"Pssst," a shadow said, from behind a shrubbery. A young woman stepped out, scrawny, pale, and sweating. She was barefoot and wore a tattered dress.

"What the hell?" I said.

She held up a red duffel bag and hissed, "I've got them. I have the papers."

The papers...

The porch light kicked on; the garage door screeched open, and my wife appeared in the streetlight's pale wash.

"What's all this?" she said, squinting at the ground, the soda cans and coffee filters. Then up, at the woman. "And who is she? What's that she's holding?"

I stood there. Felt the dew between my toes. Searched my mind for words, phrases, some rising soliloquy. Looked to the young woman, the duffel bag. Then to my wife, past her, to the blank face of the house. Looming window-eyes. I could hear crickets sawing in the grass—or the first stirrings of music, notes twinkling.

"Well," I said. "It goes like this..."

And in rolled the fog.

Molasses

.....

My girlfriend was home from work, at least two hours late, and three inches shorter, which meant it had been a tough day. She rifled through the refrigerator, lifting a bottle of diet soda, sniffing it, frowning.

"This soda's gone bad," my girlfriend said to my clean T-shirt.

I shrugged. "Its upbringing?"

"You haven't cut the grass," she said to my clean T-shirt. My T-shirt read BOO HOO.

"Grass," I said. "As if it's one big lump of lime Jell-O. I mean it's Bermuda and Fescue and St. Augustine, not to mention all the wildflowers. St. Augustine, come on, that's a story. What do you think about St. Augustine?"

"I don't," she said over a shoulder, on the way to the living room.

Long hours isn't just an expression, understand? Anything can change, under the wrong circumstances. Channels change. The television sat on its stand like a giant cube of sugar. I could hear it squawking, so I went outside.

The lawn was certainly tall, spongy beneath my feet, tendrils of grass tickling my ankles. Fallen leaves sat atop it like rafts on a green sea. Glazed biscuits squatted low, parting the blades with their doughy domes. I reached for one, then noticed it was a mushroom. I was out of molasses anyway.

The lawnmower gave me a don't-even-think-about-it look. A gust of wind leapt the fence, followed by a tree limb bending, yawning, cracking, and falling onto my crow-sketching shed.

Confused, I stared at my feet.

What if you looked closely at a lawn?

You would see wedges and spoons and slivers and beards and pebbles and broccolis and fans and straws and hearts of grass. If I could name the entire flora I would. But I can't.

I can name sunflower and dandelion and bloodroot and trillium and verbena. I can name wild potato vine. Like a river map, wild potato vine crept along the side of my crow-hunting shed.

A voice reached me from the end of the yard, then a swishing of Carolina lilies. Someone was wading Jangly Creek. Wearing oversized waders and the bowl of a pasta strainer atop her head, it was Joey.

Joey was a girl from the country who was always wading Jangly Creek into the city and selling people things from an inner tube she pulled behind her. The inner tube was once the lungs of a tractor, but no more. It now had fence slats and feed bags laid across, and held all types of useful things—shuttlecocks, disposable cameras, Play-Doh molds, and so on—things Joey found discarded, including a functional abacus, which is really quite rare.

"How are things?" I asked.

"Soapy." Joey nodded to the water. "Someone spilt something, something neon and soapy. The fish are sinking. The beavers won't gnaw. They're hiding. I haven't seen a woodchuck for days."

"Ah," I said, putting my hands to my ears. "I don't suppose you have my barley?"

"And your yeast." She handed over two recycled microwave popcorn bags, then snapped a few beads on the abacus. She had silly quick hands.

"A dollar and a half," she said.

I gave Joey two dollars and told her she could keep the change if she could tell me about St. Augustine. She nodded and searched the burlap bags, finally producing a deck of playing cards. Shuffling, then squinting at the cards, she said, "Born 13 November, 354. Lived a worldly life of wickedness and false beliefs, had a mistress or three. Then got religion. Developed ideas of original sin and predestination. Considered the patron saint of brewers."

"You're joking."

"I never joke," Joey replied, squirreling the cards away. She rubbed her nose with the business end of a flyswatter. I never saw where it came from. Or where it went. Silly quick, I'm telling you.

We visited awhile. I told Joey how my girlfriend won employee of the decade and the way my stomach fluttered last week as I watched her fingers prying ice cubes from the tray, and Joey told me about how she kept finding oil filters and bottles of water in Jangly Creek and how her father's crops were doing and what the crows were up to. Joey was my crow intelligence. The crows were ignoring the corn. They were feeding off the highways, off the shoulders and the medians. The crows were circling the malls.

"I've never seen that," I said.

She said, "When's the last time you were in town?"

"Few months ago, I guess." For some reason, I nodded to the water, at a half-eaten chicken finger floating past. "I was in Harvy's for a jar of molasses."

Joey lifted her towrope and squinted into the sun off the water. "Harvy's closed last week. One of them giant syrup stores opened right across the street; sells every kinda syrup in the world, and cheap. Harvy's gone."

"No," I said, mostly just to hear the word. Harvy made his molasses in the old way, a low fire and boiling pots of sugar. He was an artisan of molasses, and I would miss him. Shaking her head, Joey pulled her inner tube down the winding creek, her legs parting the current, the inner tube riding dark and high, their shadow some mythical creature kidnapping an island nation. I watched her round the corner and collected my bags of yeast and barley and I swear each one of them weighed ten thousand pounds.

Wal-Mart

.....

The phone I bought at Wal-Mart rings and I pick it up and Bear says, "I'm gonna kill you you skinny freshman motherfucker!"

I hang up the phone.

My stomach feels like: #$@%!

All I have to say—should you sit on your dorm room bed shivering, with a feeling of smallness and dread, with a stomach flopping like a halibut in an ice chest, with a large eggplant-faced man who goes by the nickname of Bear outside your door banging away to get in, to harm you, to stomp you, to rip you to "fucking shit-shreds," without any idea of what to do, without any real hope of personal survival, while you glance about frantically for some type of weapon (which you do not have), while you shake and grit and fight a storm-surging need to vomit—all I have to say is to be very, very quiet. If Bear doesn't hear you he might eventually *go away* and *hibernate.*

Of course I talk to the guy.

"I don't know a girl named Kristen!" I shout. (I do.)

"I never touched her!" I shout. (I did.)

Hours later I sprawl out on my bed, staring at the ceiling tiles. I'm driftwood, desensitized to the waves of sound. I can hear rain on the roof, a pattering like a giant herd of tiny, tiny horses running circles of free-living gallop. I can hear Bear, still out there, cursing, frothing, clawing at the knob, pawing at the base of the door, searching for grubs.

For the manyteenth time, I shout, "I don't know your girlfriend!"

Bear goes back to throwing his body against the door: *Doomp! Doomp! Doomp!* I find myself proud of my university's door budget, which seems large and strong. I whisper up to the peephole. Bear is huge. Bear fills the magnified hallway like eighteen tomorrows of pain. I return to my bed and stare at the ceiling.

I phone the front desk. "There's a maniac at my door."

"What did you do to him?"

I hang up and long distance my dad. He says, "Go to Wal-Mart and buy a baseball bat."

I hang up. I feel a lump rising in my side like a ruptured appendix cirrhosis tumor of worry. I think about opening the door, which would be suicide. It is not often that I consider suicide because, to be honest, I always think there might be something better about to happen, but I'm having trouble thinking that now. Then something better happens: Bear leaves.

Things should have a point, they say, or vexing questions exist.

They: I'm assuming you saw Bear again.

Me: A week later. I saw him in front of the library and he saw me and nodded his gigantical head and walked on past like I was a landscaped bed of tulips.

They: Obviously, you never saw Kristen again. And Bear never saw her again. She'd never told a soul about a man named Bear, had she?"

Me: You're very intuitive.

They: She probably wasn't even his girlfriend, but rather his—

Me: Fiancée.

They: Right . . .Do you think life needs metaphors?

Me: No.

They: Me neither. Final question. Did you return the bat to Wal-Mart?

Me: Yes, weeks later. I didn't even have a receipt. They were very nice about it. I love Wal-Mart. All of us love Wal-Mart.

How Some People Like Their Eggs

.....

General Patton:

He orders his eggs like his battles, pitched. Eats them fast off the plate—fork, mouth, fork, mouth—with no condiments. Finishes them off with a room temperature beer (learned that in Luxembourg). Picks up his hat. Stands tall and shouts, "Thank you, egg, this morning! You genius bastard do-your-damndest chicken coffin son-of-a-bitch!" Looks around and nods. Places his hat. Winks at a girl on a wall calendar. Marches outside. Salutes the sun, and if there is no sun, salutes a cloud in the shape of malaria.

Yogi Berra:

Doesn't eat eggs anymore. "No one does," he says, with a shrug. "You can't find them at the grocery. They're always sold out."

Billie Holiday:

Served Sunny Side Up, inverted. Like two dreams dropped from a great height. Big and round and shiny and flat. Served with a glass of rusty tap water. Served fourteen minutes after cooking. While cooling. While cool.

Andy Warhol:
Upstairs, on the paint-spattered floor, an eight-step process. He:

1. wakes.
2. checks to see if anyone has stolen his Sony Walkman. No one has.
3. finds this grainy video (an old SX-70 camera; smeared a layer of Vaseline and cigarette ash on the lens) of Marilyn Monroe digging the cotton from an asthma inhaler and eating it with a loopy smile.
4. Freezes the video and takes a photo of the TV screen with a Polaroid and then drops the developed image into a pan of milk.
5. heats the milk on a hotplate.
6. tweezes the photo from the saucer.
7. uses three Q-tips and a burnishing tool to manipulate the emulsion inside the Polaroid.
8. admires the unexpected surprise of the TV lines (monitor phosphors caught on film), but finds the final image less than pleasing. Less than art, certainly. So he smokes two low-tar cigarettes, poaches an egg—eats it.

Howard Hughes:
Steam-basted. In an autoclave.

Bonnie Parker:
However Clyde wants them. But he don't want them at all. He wants a Baby Ruth for breakfast. Three of them, and a chocolate malt; and so he drives the Ford V8 hard to Dallas. She thinks about eggs, a poem of eggs, to write in her red notebook: *White hens, white eggs. Red hens, brown. A good egg floats, a bad one sinks. The moon is a floating egg, yellow light on the fields, square-shouldered...* "What you thinking on?" Clyde says, swerves to hit a scrawny beagle crossing the road, misses, belches, and tosses a milk bottle out the window. "Nothing," she answers. "I'm just hungry."

Archduke Franz Ferdinand Karl Anikò Belschwitz Mòric Bálint Szilveszter Gömpi Bzoch János Frajkor Ludwig Josef von Habsburg-Lothringen of Austria:
Franz invites a Slav to breakfast. Then a Croat, a Serb, a German. All decline. He sits alone in his castle, glances around and thinks: *Why do others seem to have more friends? And the friends I have, even they seem distant. Or does it only appear that way?* Sophie rides up on a horse and carriage and this makes Franz's heart go all Mylar balloon: shiny and floating and free. "Please don't go to Bosnia," she pleads, and places a newspaper and a goose egg on the table. "They want to kill you in Bosnia." "I-am-going-to-Bosnia!" Franz declares. The egg is boiled.

Anne Sexton:

She rises early, for domestic chores. Vacuums the air of dust motes. Wet mops the ceiling. While her family sleeps in their well-made beds, she fries their eggs, occasionally nibbling the crisping edges, the whites. She thinks: *Here I am again.* She thinks: *What word possibly rhymes with spatula?* She listens to the refrigerator hum. The freezer hum. Her own humming. Then she pierces the yolks; they bloom and bleed: a peony, a water clock, a lioness clutching at a crow.

Che Guevara:

Che likes a bold omelet. He'll add anything: asparagus tips, bread, a handful of spare change. He was the first to think: clarified butter. He eats on a promontory, above the Gulf Stream, alone. An attractive girl walks up and takes a photo of his head.

Robert Capa:

Mr. Capa tries to cook his eggs on an outdoor grill. It cannot be done. He stumbles inside, to the kitchen. The phone rings. He answers and someone yells, "How dare you wear that helmet in public! That's GI issue. You took it off a dead man!" Capa throws the phone down, the cord coiling about his leg like a snake. He sits and thinks about sex, where to get some. Sits in the nude and eats his eggs runny, with a chaser of Polish vodka. On a tin plate inscribed with the words: "Property of Robert Capa, great war correspondent and lover."

Cher:
Coddled eggs.

Buzz Aldrin:
Looks at the clock. Phones up Armstrong; says, "You had breakfast yet?" Armstrong answers, "Hours ago, my man." Buzz hangs up with a sigh. Pushes his eggs around the plate. They are raw.

Thelonious Monk:
No human being knows how Thelonious Monk likes his eggs.

Crow Hunting

.....

Wednesdays seem a day to reflect. A day for gentler things. It's their personality—the misshapen nature, the hump, the way a Wednesday morning feels like the last sip of home-brewed beer. Silty.

Wednesdays were a kind of holiday. My crow-hunting day.

With a high-step past the dozing mower, I approached my crow-hunting shed. Scattered around the shed were rows of sprouting trees, mostly pine. Bending down, I snapped off a twig and sniffed its sweet odor.

Crisp, uplifting, green.

I could easily inhale the odor of pine all day.

But this was Wednesday, so I turned to the shed's padlock. It was a copper lock and to open it you had to sigh into a tiny hole in its center. I sighed and stepped inside.

I collected my art supplies and my owl decoys and several calls, the tubes dangling from their braided ropes. I wore the calls proudly, as necklaces. I had three specific calls to lure crows my way.

1. The "We're fighting the owl-of-owls over here" call.
2. The "We're feeding like politicians on parade over here" call.
3. The death call.

Crows are social beings, and extremely intelligent.

Here's how I hunted them:

I climbed bamboo trees until they bent in half and I rode them to the ground like a pole vaulter, only in reverse. I placed owl decoys atop the trees and let them fling upright. They looked like Christmas tree angels. I got my sketchpad and a six pack of home-brewed beer and hid beneath a cathedral of camo netting.

Then I called.

My first call said, "Brute horror and talons and act, oh, air, hate, plume—attack! A great horned owl eating eggs. Making omelets. Making eggnog, touch of nutmeg. With the feathers of our brood, making flapjacks."

My second call said, "Rolling level underneath, combine shudders, corn popping nuggets of gold. Gold! Earrings of gold have fallen from the corn's ear—combine shudders!"

Pleasantly sipping my beer, I knelt in the high weeds and looked into the sky. It was full of clouds and one of the clouds resembled Alaska. A crow appeared above Prince William's Sound, gliding into Anchorage, veering north toward Mount McKinley.

It was the scout crow so I had two options.

1. Let it pass, since a scout crow, unless sketched perfectly, will warn the entire flock of a human's presence.
2. Sketch it perfectly.

I let the crow pass.

And the flock appeared, attacking the owl decoys, ripping into their synthetic souls. Then sensing the owl's plasticity, the crows ceased their attacking. They floated and perched, cawing, gossiping to one another, and I scribbled along, pondering their tidbits.

"Long as my rent gets paid by Sunday."

" . . .can't be expected to fly under such conditions."

"She gave him that kimono."

" . . .a kilo of first-class New Orleans seed."

" . . .under apple trees by the river."

For several hundred minutes, I made my careful drawings. The tip of my pencil wore down and eventually passed away. I set the pencil down and drank my beer, and watched the crows. One crow cawing, simply cawing. One crow off by itself, sharpening its beak on a clothesline pole, reminiscing of a plum it dropped over West Virginia. Two crows bobbing in rhythm on a pine bough. One crow doing aerial eights, while another cuts through the loops, creating its own eight, then another, linking together, sixteen, twenty-four, thirty-two . . .

Marvelous, my beer-soaked mind thought, borrowing my mouth to whisper, "Marvelous."

Once the crows detect a human—once alarmed and on their way—you use the death call. It sounds like

rippling of bones
around
them

It says, "I'm dying, right now, and will you help me?" As true as Wednesday, the crows reappear, and you get that final image, spiraling frame, buckling of wings and heart, the curvature of returning. But I never use the death call.

Coffee Pot Tree

.....

With hearts of eggshell and blue we finally had the old Coffee Pot Tree down; it had been a loyal pal, giving us shade and conversation and a synapse-drenching amount of quality caffeine, but had become a neighborhood bother, a tramp in plain sight, an arthritic beggar who no longer had the common decency to avert his eyes, a general menace to suburban equilibrium, drooping over the front lawn, threatening the children, the smaller dogs, the domestic rodents (squirrels, chipmunks), dangling its French presses and stainless percolators and espresso/cappuccino machines in a manner hardly conducive to the workings of our little society.

"It will have to come down," one of our more serious neighbors declared, one hand planted firmly on hip, the other shielding her eyes from the afternoon sun off the burnished sides of the coffee makers. (I say declared since veiled within her words was the simple fact she held the post of secretary for the Neighborhood Advisory and Recreation Committee [NARC] and could certainly arrange a meeting, a vote, a predictable result of said vote.)

I didn't argue; I seldom do anymore.

Not fourteen days after the tree came down, after the wife and I paid to have it topped, dropped, and carted away, I was winterizing the lawn and stumbled upon a wayward pot, an automatic drip, with a crack down its side in the shape of a question mark. I held it aloft like some archeological find, hefted it high, its weight solid and reassuring. And then my nose caught a sweet, rich aroma, my ears a gentle hissing—in the cavern of the pot, a twirl of lively coffee, a bubbling verve, perseverance, some warm hope of life.

I thought of only days ago, of how the clouds would thicken above the satellite dishes, the leaves scuttle in the breeze, and I would silence the leaf blower and listen: the Coffee Pot Tree suddenly a wind chime, pealing clear like church bells, the shrug and kiss of metal and glass, the gurgle of percolation.

But that was days ago, and what is days ago but weeks ago but years ago but now? This is how my mind meandered; these thoughts as I took, and swirled in my mouth, the final hot sip of the only coffee I'd ever known, and then of how much the world must truly suffer its serious people.

Endings

.....

A couple takes a dog for a walk along a rain-swollen Potomac River. The man throws a stick into the water, and the woman, unaware, lobs a tennis ball. The dog leaps from the bank, swims to the stick, to the ball, to the stick, a desperate orbit, and all the while the current tugging him downstream and around a corner. The man shouts several things, his words snatched away by the wind. The woman falls to her knees. On the way home they either stop by Starbucks, run out of gas, or explode.

Alabama Highway 59. An overweight Eagle Scout pulls over to help change a woman's tire. The humidity is such that the young man feels submerged in a boiling pot. The word *lobster* comes to mind. As his sweaty hands struggle with a lug nut, he is swiped by a semi and killed.

Swarming honeybees are subdued by smoke. They are then trained to sniff out plastic explosives. Instead they spend their time creating geometrically accurate octagons. For this, the bees are heralded as evidence of intelligent design, or caught in Mason jars, suffocated, and fed to laboratory mice in West Virginia—or both.

A teenage girl catches an amazingly large fish. She pauses, allowing herself to gaze in wonder. It has a row of bent hooks and five broken leaders in its mouth. It has a history. The girl isn't really a girl. She only plays one online. She is actually a grown man who works in a chemical company that combines corn husks with hydrochloric acid to create a polymer used in cruise missiles. He bashes the head of the fish on the gunwale and tosses it thrashing into an Igloo cooler.

Denny goes to an art gallery in downtown Cincinnati, mostly to impress an extremely cute hipster girl. He notes all of the photos are of crows. Crows on electrical wires. Crows perched on a scarecrow's arm. Crows feeding, eating French fries, gum, a ruptured bag of Cheetos. When did all the crows start feeding in parking lots? The girl meets a friend at the gallery, another girl, and leaves in a cab. Denny walks to a nearby rooftop bar and drinks so many beers he feels his legs floating. Soaring higher...and so he flies.

A ferret twists frees from the arms of his owner and runs directly into a passing train.

Sandy works at this bait shop in Upper Michigan. A senior citizen pulls out a filet knife and demands a Styrofoam minnow bucket, for free. He carves the air with his bony fingers. Sandy selects a large revolver (one of many secreted throughout the store) from behind the register, and says: "Old man. We all could use a better understanding of our situations." Then she shoots him in the forehead.

About the Author

.....

Sean Lovelace is a professor of creative writing at Ball State University. He writes fiction, poetry, and creative nonfiction. Recent publications include *Willow Springs, Diagram, Sonora Review,* and *Black Warrior Review*. His works have won several awards, including the prestigious *Crazyhorse* Fiction Prize. He blogs at seanlovelace.com. He also likes to run, far.

A Note About the Type

.....

The interior of this book is set in Mrs Eaves. Designed by Zuzana Licko in 1996, the typeface was inspired by John Baskerville's transitional eighteenth-century typefaces and takes its name from Baskerville's housekeeper turned wife, Sarah Eaves. The fancifully named type has a small x-height and body, which give it a light and airy feel. Contemporary critics of Baskerville's designs accused him of hurting readers' eyes with his high contrast types; with her revival, Licko aimed to reduce contrast and widen the letterforms while retaining a feeling of openness.

The cover uses Mrs Eaves and Chalet Comprimé, a font based on the experimental typeface designs by French fashion designer André Albert Chalet.

—Heather Butterfield